NEIL POSTMAN

CRAZY TALK, STUPID TALK

How We Defeat Ourselves
by the Way We Talk—
and What to Do About It

A DELTA BOOK

A Delta Book
Published by
Dell Publishing Co., Inc.
1 Dag Hammarskjold Plaza
New York, New York 10017

ISBN: 0-440-51549-1

Published by arrangement with Delacorte Press
Printed in the United States of America
First Delta printing—August 1977

"One should, each day, try to hear a little song, read a good poem, see a fine picture, and, if it is possible, speak a few reasonable words."

Goethe

Contents

Foreword

This is a book about talk. Not every kind of talk, but the kind which I think it useful and virtuous to expose as crazy or stupid. I do not believe there exists a technical definition of either of these accusations, but if there does, I am not using it here. Stupid talk, as I mean the phrase, is talk that has (among other difficulties) a confused direction or an inappropriate tone or a vocabulary not well-suited to its context. It is talk, therefore, that does not and cannot achieve its purposes. To accuse people of stupid talk is to accuse them of using language ineffectively, of having made harmful but correctable mistakes in performance. It is a serious matter, but not usually dreadful.

Crazy talk is something else and is almost always dreadful. As I will use the phrase, crazy talk is talk that may be entirely effective but which has unreasonable or evil or, sometimes, overwhelmingly trivial purposes. It is talk that creates an irrational context for itself or sustains an irrational conception of human interaction. It, too, is correctable, but only by improving our values, not our competence.

What I am investigating in this book is how, through lack of knowledge, awareness, or discipline, we frequently talk both crazy and stupid and thereby create mischief and pain. The purpose of the book is to indicate how we can reduce such talk to tolerable levels, so that our verbal behavior will not be an excessive burden to ourselves and others.

This is no easy matter to do. The subject is filled with complexity, contradiction, and general confusion. For example, on the day I am writing these words, there is a story in the newspapers about the late J. Edgar Hoover. It informs us that Hoover's car was once struck from behind while "it" was making a left turn. As a consequence, Hoover forbade all left turns on any of his automobile trips, including trips of several hundred miles.

Assuming the political pun to be irrelevant here, how could one have persuaded Mr. Hoover that there was something "wrong" with the way he had formulated his problem? Do you suppose it would have made a difference if someone had explained to him that cars do not make left turns, only drivers do? And that one bad turn does not foretell another? Or that the usual 10-minute trip from the FBI building to his favorite Washington restaurant would, under his rules, now take him through Norwalk, Connecticut? I doubt it, and for a few reasons.

The first is that the process of "anthropomorphizing"— of attributing human qualities to inanimate objects, such as cars—is a very difficult speech habit to break. It is more than likely that Hoover was partial to this habit and would not have found it easy to eliminate from his strategies for thinking. The second is that we are all somewhat in love with our ways of talking about the world, whatever deformities such talk might have, and it takes some doing to convince any of us that our favorite sentences often betray our best interests. But even more important, on what grounds could we argue that our sense of the problem is more legitimate than his? Hoover, obviously, thought his problem was cars that make left turns. *We* can see, I assume, that his problem had to do with directions of thinking/talking, not turning. What is the standard which gives us the authority to instruct him? Who is to say which of us is seeing the matter correctly? You'll be pleased to know that there *are* standards by which to judge these matters, and, if I have done this book right, these will be visible to you before long.

Meanwhile, here is another sort of problem of the type to which we will have to address ourselves. A few years ago Richard Nixon put forward a man by the name of Clement Haynsworth to fill a vacancy on the Supreme Court. It was agreed by everyone that Haynsworth was in every sense a mediocre candidate. He had certainly been a mediocre lawyer and judge. In arguing for Haynsworth's appointment, Roman Hruska (presently Senator from Nebraska) remarked with serious intent that since there were so many mediocre people in America they were entitled to be represented by a mediocre Supreme Court justice.

Now this application of the language of representative government has many rich possibilities. One might argue, for example, that America needs mediocre brain surgeons to operate on all those people with mediocre brains. Or, Richard Nixon, on the basis of this sort of reasoning, could have defended himself by arguing that since there are so many criminals in America they deserve to be represented by a President who is himself a criminal.

In any case, I think you can see that this type of thinking can generate a considerable amount of stupid talk. Is there any way to change Senator Hruska's point of view by making him more aware of his language? I think there is. Our language structures the very way we see, and any significant change in our ways of talking can lead to a change in point of view. Nonetheless, stupid and crazy talk is a large and even mysterious subject, and one has to approach it with a proper respect for the idiosyncrasies of human perception.

With this in mind, I intend to show how one may proceed in approaching the subject—what questions need to be asked, what considerations must be given, what criteria may reasonably be used to avoid the mismanagement of our thinking/talking.

Obviously, then, there's a question you will want to have answered before going any further: By what authority do I write such a book? (I am, after all, claiming special knowledge in a very broad area of human behavior.) I have five answers to this question, but only the last of them is any good. The first three are, themselves, excellent examples of stupid talk. In order, here they are: I am a professor of communication at New York University. I have written previously on this subject. I have been given awards testifying that I know what I am talking about. (This one was suggested to me by the Wizard of Oz.)

The fourth is not quite so obviously stupid, although it is far from convincing: I have spent fifteen years making systematic observations of how people talk and trying to explain to myself why talk so often confounds our purposes. Please note the *nature* of the question I have been asking. I have not been trying to find out what "intelligent" talk is. I have been trying to find out what "dumb" talk is. In this respect, I have modeled my inquiries after those of doctors and lawyers. What is the first question a doctor (or a lawyer) will ask you when you seek his or her advice? It is something like, "What's the trouble?" Even the wisest of them cannot tell you what good health is or what justice is. They can only say what bad health is and whether or not an injustice has been done. We might even say that, to a doctor, good health is the absence of bad health; to a lawyer, justice is the absence of injustice. Some people say that this is not the right way to look at the matter. And perhaps they are correct. But I know very few people who will consult a doctor to get an opinion on what is good health. And I know even fewer who will approach a lawyer to find out what justice is. In any case, in my own inquiries into talk, I have discovered that the varieties of effective, purpose-enhancing talk are so diverse and unpredictable as to defy classification. Not so the varieties of destructive talk. Like illnesses and injuries, they are identifiable, their properties are discussable, and I have reason to believe that, within limits, they are reducible.

Which leads me to the fifth and final answer to the question: By what authority do I write this book? The answer is the book itself. If you find that its perspective is usable in helping you manage your language affairs, then, for you, the book may be considered authoritative and its author, an authority. If you do not find it so, then there is no help for me. My professorship, previous writings, awards, and research will not protect me from the charge that I have wasted your time. But assuming you find the book useful, there is still another question you might want answered before going on: What is the theoretical basis of my approach to the problem?

There are, of course, no chairs for the Study of Stupid Talk in our universities, and no one has ever received a Nobel Prize for uncovering the underlying structure of crazy talk. Perhaps someday crazy talk and stupid talk will be considered important enough to make into a subject in our schools—let us say, at least as important as public speaking or business administration or Elizabethan nondramatic literature. Meanwhile, those of us interested in the matter must find our ideas wherever we can. In my case, this has meant turning to people such as Karl Popper, George Herbert Mead, Alfred Korzybski, I. A. Richards, George Orwell, Lewis Mumford, Gregory Bateson, Wendell Johnson, Kenneth Burke, and Saul Alinsky. You may be relieved to know I have not cluttered the text with elaborate explanations of how I am using their ideas, especially since I no longer know what I have taken from them. I do, however, and most emphatically, relieve them of all responsibility for such stupidities as you may find in the text.

And speaking of the text, you may find it useful to know that it is divided into three parts. In Part 1, I try to put forward the general framework of the "problem," including, toward the end, a relatively clear distinction between crazy talk and stupid talk. Part 2

consists of seventeen small chapters, each of which identifies and tries to explain a particular characteristic of
such talk. These characteristics include certain beliefs,
speech habits, and structural aspects of language which,
if not carefully controlled, lead us into talking crazy or
stupid. Part 3 is a single chapter in which I try to
suggest a point of view we may adopt which, it seems
to me, will help us to keep well clear of such talk.

Finally, this is probably the place for me to clarify a
certain semantic point which, if left murky, may cause
trouble. Several writers have pointed out that roughly
one-third of all the verbs we use in normal discourse are
some form of the verb *to be*, and, further, that there are
some forms of it that are exceedingly cunning in con-
founding our understanding. One of these is sometimes
called the *is* of projection, as in the sentence "He is
stupid." What is mysterious about this sentence is that
through a kind of grammatical alchemy it creates the
impression that stupidity is an innate property of whom-
ever you are talking about, like, for example, the person's
height or weight or eye color. But stupidity is no such
thing. It is a behavior, done at a particular time and in
particular circumstances. This means that in discussing
stupidity, we are not talking about those who "have" it
and those who don't. We are talking about the ways in
which people "do" stupidity. One can even do stupidity
or craziness on purpose in order to achieve certain rational ends. For example, I have seen men in the army
go into well-practiced stupid routines in order to avoid
being chosen for odious tasks. I have also seen both men
and women do the same, and for the same reason, in
domestic settings. And it is by no means rare for a child

to do this in school. (Paul Goodman called this "reactive stupidity.") But in these cases, the doer has himself under control. It is the situation that is out of his control. What I mean by control is a thorough awareness of what is going on in a situation, including your own responses to it. But what we are concerned with in this book is doing stupidity or craziness when it is not what you intended or, if it is, doing it with hideous consequences to someone else.

PART

1

The Semantic Environment

Stupidity is words. It is not something people "possess," like their kidneys. Stupidity is something we *speak*, sentences that do not "make sense" or are self-defeating. We may speak such sentences to others or only to ourselves. But the point is that stupidity is something we do with our larynx.

What our larynx does is controlled by the way we manage our minds. No one knows, of course, what "mind" is, and there are even those who think it wise to avoid discussing it altogether. But this much we can say: The main stuff of the mind is sentences. "Minding" and "languaging" are, for all practical purposes, one and the same. When we are thinking, we are mostly arranging sentences in our heads. When we are thinking stupid, we are arranging stupid sentences.

I will go so far as to say that the entire subject matter of stupidity is encompassed by the study of our ways of talking. Even when we do a nonverbal stupid thing, like

smoking a cigarette (one of my own cherished stupidities), we have preceded the act by talking to ourselves
in such a way as to make it appear reasonable. One might
say that stupid talk is the generative act from which all
the Higher Stupidities flow. The word, in a word, brings
forth the act.

Moreover, stupidity is something of a linguistic achievement. It does not, I believe, come naturally to us. We
must learn how to do it, and practice how to do it. Naturally, once having learned and practiced it, we find it
difficult, possibly painful, to forget how to do it. Speaking, after all, is a habit, and habits, by definition, are
hard to break.

Craziness is much the same thing. Crazy behavior is
produced by our generating certain kinds of sentences
which we have nurtured and grown to love. When, for
example, Lynette Fromme was sentenced to life impris-
onment for attempting to assassinate Gerald Ford, she
said, "I want [Charles] Manson out. I want a world of
peace." Considering the hideous circumstances by which
Manson came to be imprisoned, and considering what
most people mean by "peace," you might say that Ms.
Fromme exhibited an almost wondrous creativity in putting those two sentences together. We can fairly assume
that she sees a connection between them. There are, no
doubt, several unspoken sentences by which she has
formed a bridge between Manson and *peace*. Even further, there must be still more sentences by which she
connects Manson and peace to the assassination of Ford.
Crazy acts are not illogical to those who do them. But
the point is that in order to do them, you must first build
a verbal empire of intricate dimension. A great deal of

crazy talk must be processed before assassination will appear as a reasonable thing to do.

And so, this book is an inquiry into some of the dimensions of stupid and crazy talk, two of our older nemeses. But let me make no bones about what is going on here: Stupid and crazy talk are not "objective" facts, like a disease or a famine or a war. They are accusations made by one individual about the talking behavior of another or a group of others. They are labels—a taxonomy of ridicule—by which a person denounces what he believes is an inappropriate way to speak and, therefore, to conduct oneself.

Thus, to condemn the way people talk is a form of personal and cultural criticism, its value depending on the knowledge and art of the critic, as well as the seriousness of his point of view. For reasons which are not entirely clear to me, there are critics of talk who fix their attention on the way people enunciate, or on how they pronounce their words, or on their standard deviations from grammatical propriety. This, too, is an exercise in cultural criticism but, in my opinion, of such a trivial nature that it is a wonder that anyone does it. If Lynette Fromme had said, "I wants Manson out. I wants a world of peace," we could scarcely improve her or ourselves by reviewing the rules of grammatical concordance. We would still be faced with the question: What are the sentences in her head that led her to connect these two desires and then connect them with the prospect of a fallen Gerald Ford? Although there are some circumstances in which criticism of the cosmetic features of language may have substance, in general I suspect that the critic who is preoccupied with it has not thought deeply on the subject. To paraphrase a remark by I. A. Richards (about superficiality in the criticism of poetry), we pay attention to externals when we are at a loss for anything else to say.

In any event, the road taken here is one that has previously been traveled by critics who were willing to set standards, not of pronunciation and grammar, but of purpose and meaning and, indeed, reason itself. But what is reason? And how do we know when it has been breached? And in what circumstances can we do without it? And is "reasonableness" the same in all situations?

These are some of the questions which have been addressed by the most serious critics of language and thought—Wittgenstein, Richards, Dewey, Korzybski, Orwell, to name a few. They have been willing to offer us rules for managing our thought, rules of semantic order, rules (if you will) for avoiding stupid or crazy talk. Some of their advice has been (in my opinion) unimpeachable, but some of it seems to me quite suspicious. For example, in his famous essay "Politics and the English Language," George Orwell offered some forthright rules which he hoped people would follow as a means of improving their use of language and, therefore, their ways of behaving themselves. Included among these rules is the advice never to use a long word where a short one will do; never to use a metaphor which you are used to seeing in print, and never to use a foreign phrase or scientific word if you can think of an everyday equivalent. If we merely simplify our language, Orwell told us, we will know when we are talking nonsense. To quote him, "When you make a stupid remark, its stupidity will be obvious, even to yourself."

Now, this has got to be one of the stupidest remarks

George Orwell ever committed to print. In fact, it is self-canceling, since if it is true, then why wasn't Orwell aware of how stupid his remark was? The answer is that the statement isn't true. One's own stupidity is almost never self-evident, even when you have become accustomed to using original, short, and everyday words, and even if you have faithfully read George Orwell. It may be a good idea (sometimes) to use short words instead of long ones or everyday words instead of obscure ones, but the problem of recognizing one's own stupidities, as well as someone else's, goes much deeper than Orwell's advice suggests. We may, indeed, learn to recognize stupid talk, but it is not accomplished by obedience to a few simple rules, as Orwell, incidentally, knew perfectly well.

What is wrong with Orwell's advice is that it is unecological. It places language outside of any context in which it is used. And by so doing, it falsifies the real process by which our judgments—Is this smart? dumb? sane? crazy?—are made. Here is a small example of what I mean by unecological: I once had to give a speech in Darien, Connecticut. When I arrived at the auditorium where it was to take place, my host looked at his watch, noted the time of my arrival, and then said, "You certainly made good time in getting here." Now, this was impossible for him to know since he was unaware of a) where I had started from and b) what time I had left. By knowing only when I had arrived, he did not *know enough* to judge whether or not I had made good time. It is the same with stupid or crazy talk. By knowing only what someone has said, we do not know enough to judge even its meaning, let alone its quality. To determine that, we must take into account what I am going to call the semantic environment.

Now, the idea of a semantic environment will not easily make sense to you if you are strongly inclined toward the "Ping-Pong ball" theory of communication (as many people seem to be). In the Ping-Pong ball theory, communication is conceived of as a discrete, quantifiable piece of stuff that will move from one source to another and then back. I say something to you, you then say something to me, I reply, you come back with another message, and so on. It is as if two machines were conversing—playing with words, so to speak—each taking its turn in delivering a message. That is the trouble, of course, with the theory. It treats people as if they were machines, and makes the study of communication a branch of classical physics. People become "sources," their words become "message units," and their purposes and situation become irrelevant. Our attention gets directed to such matters as the quantity of messages, the force of messages, the speed of messages, the efficiency of receptors, and so on. And when we seek advice on how to communicate better, the theory tells us to make our messages shorter, or slower, or more familiar, or more redundant. In the Ping-Pong ball theory, it is not even necessary to distinguish between machine–machine talk and people–people talk.

The metaphor of a semantic environment invites an entirely different view of the matter. It says that communication is not stuff or bits or messages. In a way, it is not even something that people do. Communication is a situation in which people participate, rather like the way a plant participates in what we call its growth. A plant does not exactly grow because it *does* something. Growth is a consequence of complex transactions among the plant, the soil, the air, the sun, and water. All in the proper proportions, at the proper time, according to the proper rules. If there is no sun or water, there is nothing much the plant can do about growing. And if there is no semantic environment, there is nothing much we can do about communicating. If communication is to happen, we require not merely messages, but an ordered situation in which messages can assume meaning.

Therefore, a semantic environment includes, first of all, people; second, their purposes; third, the general rules of discourse by which such purposes are usually achieved; and fourth, the particular talk actually being used in the situation. There is much more to it than this, as I hope to show, but for the moment, let's say there are these four elements. Now, because there are so many different kinds of roles for people to play and so many different human purposes, there are many kinds of semantic environments, each with special rules by which people are expected to conduct themselves. Science is a semantic environment. So is politics, commerce, war, sports, religion, lovemaking, law making, among others. Each of these situations is a social structure in which people want to do something to, for, with, or against other people, as well as to, for, with, or against themselves. I am referring to those semantic environments which give form to our most important human transactions. Moreover, within any one of these semantic environments, there are many subenvironments which, when taken together, comprise the larger environment.

For example, the Confessional is a semantic environment within the larger semantic environment of religion. To judge whether or not someone's verbal conduct is stupid or crazy, one must have some knowledge not only of the rules of discourse of a subenvironment (e.g., the Confessional) but also of the larger environment of which it is a part (i.e., religion). The words "Father, I have sinned" can be judged perfectly reasonable when uttered inside a box that is inside a church to a man who wears a special garment and is pledged to secrecy. But the same words come out stupid talk when uttered inside an office-building elevator to a man who is reading *Popular Mechanics* and is on his way to the dentist. So the first thing we need to recognize is that in thinking about talk, we are dealing with a multifaceted social situation. What makes crazy talk crazy or stupid talk stupid is not the language people use but *the relationship of their remarks to the totality of the situation they are in*. And that totality always includes people, purposes, principles, and performance.

And so our first problem is to identify in a general way the type of semantic environment we are dealing with. Unless we know that, we can scarcely say anything about the sanity or wisdom of people's language behavior.

Now, sometimes it is very easy to tell what sort of situation people are in, and sometimes it is not. A man in a witness box or a confessional box or a batter's box has already shown you almost all you need to know about the situation he is in; it should not be difficult to guess what sort of sentences ought to come out of his mouth. The purposes and rules of such situations are fairly well known, and the batter, for example, who turns to the umpire and says, "Father, I have sinned . . ." is either trying to make a bad joke or needs a psychiatrist more than a priest or an umpire. A man in a witness box is in an even more rigorously ordered semantic environment than the ball field. In fact, a courtroom is one of the few environments in our society where there is an official umpire whose job is to monitor the appropriateness of the remarks people make. In most other situations, the "umpire" is not a specially trained, disinterested party but merely the person you are talking to—someone who, instead of intoning, "Your remarks are out of order," mumbles silently, "What an idiotic thing to say!" For example, imagine a young woman beginning to stir with romantic feeling on a beach in Waikiki. She sighs to her boyfriend, "Isn't that sunset gorgeous?" Now, imagine her boyfriend replying: "Well, strictly speaking, the sun is not setting. Nor does it ever do so. The sun, you see, is in a relatively fixed position in relation to the earth. So, to speak precisely, one ought to say that the earth is rising." A very good sentence for a general science class in junior high school, but an exceedingly dumb one on a beach in Waikiki, or even Rockaway—as the boyfriend will learn soon enough if he tries that sentence one more time.

But sometimes it is not so easy to know what sort of situation we are in, and then it takes some work to know how we are to construe the remarks of other people. Consider, for example, a sentence that appears in a "horoscope" column in a daily newspaper. Here is a typical but fabricated one (largely because it has proved difficult to obtain permission from horoscope writers to have their sentences analyzed): "Prepare yourself for all situa-tions, and do not act until you have considered the mat-ter fully."

Naturally, our first question is to wonder about what sort of environment we are being invited to join. Obvi-ously, we are being given advice of some sort and, as a parting shot from your father as you leave home for the first time, the advice is not all that bad. It is certainly no worse than "Know thyself" or "Neither a borrower nor a lender be." But since the column is called a "horoscope," we have reason to infer that the writer is drawing on resources not readily available to Socrates, Polonius, or other fatherly people. Even so, as a prediction of things to come or as a message from the cosmos, the advice seems to lack both precision and weight, to say the least. The writer does not do much better in addressing Sagit-tarians, who are advised to "Be calm even in the face of disappointment. Difficulties will iron themselves out." Here, the advice is rather dubious, especially the part about difficulties getting ironed. Still, one expects rather more substance than this from the stars.

And so, we now must get serious and insist on knowing exactly what is the semantic environment of which these remarks are a part. Well, we know that astrologers are inclined to represent themselves as forecasters, and there-fore, we may guess that their intention is to replicate the functions of science. If that is the case here, we've got our first really good example of stupid talk. Since the main purpose of the semantic environment called science is to produce reliable and predictable knowledge about the world, the rules of scientific discourse are fairly pre-cise. We are obliged, for example, to put our statements in such a form that they are either verifiable or refutable. We are also obliged to have our statements open to public scrutiny, to express ourselves at all times tentatively, to define our terms concretely, and to keep our language relatively free of ambiguity. This astrologer easily passes the test of public scrutiny, but on all other counts, her performance is deplorable. The closest she comes to a predictive statement is in her remarks to Taurus: "Today, there will be an unusual development. People will accept your ideas," and to Aries: "A long-hoped-for opportunity will arrive this evening." An unusual development? A long-hoped-for opportunity? Well, these could be anything, couldn't they? There is nothing here that lends itself to much verification or refutation, except in the most subjective way, and yet the writer speaks without apology or hesitation. Perhaps that is *why* she speaks without apology or hesitation. In any case, we needn't dwell too long on the point: As science, such language is stupid talk, pure and simple, and you don't need my instruction to come to this conclusion.

But suppose this language is not intended as science? In that case, the rules of scientific talk would not apply in judging it. Well, if you examine enough astrological "predictions," a reasonable alternative comes to mind. It becomes almost obvious that we are being invited to participate in a religious situation of some sort. What we are given, more or less continuously, are secular mini-sermons. To Capricorn: "Do not complicate your life. Finish what you have started." Who talks like this if not a preacher? To Leo: "Rid yourself of what you do not need." A saint might say this with more elegance but it would appear that the writer is coming much closer to the business of religion than to that of science. It is true that nowhere in this language or any other horoscope is the authority of God invoked, but an astrologer does almost as well by invoking the authority of the stars. Both God and the stars have this in common: No evidence is required to support their injunctions. What is written is written, and that is sufficient.

And so, we are drawn to the conclusion that astrologers are in the stately and profound realm of religion, and we must now ask, What are the purposes of religious talk? What are its rules? And, finally, how well do astrologers do it?

In general, we may say that the semantic environment we call religion serves, at its best, to minimize fear and isolation, to increase freedom, and to provide a sense of continuity and oneness. Religious language achieves these purposes by creating metaphors and myths which give concrete form to our most profound fears and exaltations. Above all, religious language provides people with a coherent system of principles by which they may give ethical purpose and direction to their lives.

If you will accept this hasty statement of the purposes of religious language, then perhaps you will conclude, as I do, that my hypothetical astrologer's attempt to dwell in this realm is very close to depraved. She offers her readers almost the exact opposite of what religion hopes to achieve. She gives advice, all right, but it is capricious, unprincipled, and without transcendent purpose. Her language is a reproach to Einstein: God *does* play dice with the universe, and there is no ethical reason why anyone should do anything. The saint who tells you to simplify your life and the preacher who advises you to rid yourself of what you do not need speak from a reasonably ordered point of view. They are making commentaries on some central moral doctrine. They have *reasons*. But in astrological theology, there are no reasons, which is why a reader must check every day to get new instructions. Since this is religion without an ethical basis, the reader cannot internalize a pattern of behavior and project it onto the future. The stars are just as likely to advise you to strike your neighbor's cheek as to offer your own. There is this difference between the stars and God: They both tell you what to do, but the stars do not tell you why. (God doesn't always tell you either, but even then we assume an ethical basis to His demands.)

And so I come to this conclusion: My astrologer is no linguistic fumbler. She uses simple, easily accessible words, and her advice is not difficult to follow. Put her sentences in the mouth of a minister, and most of them will make quite good sense. But for all of this, the language is crazy talk. As an expression of ethical or religious sentiment, its rules are unpredictable, its purposes suspect, its effects disintegrative. A constant reader could hardly get any other picture of the world than that it is ruled by a benign lunatic who amuses himself by sending fragments of advice to earthlings who are, at best, vague about their moral direction. In short, I am saying that the semantic environment of religion has legitimate social and psychological purposes and appropriate rules of discourse which are subverted in the most bizarre way by astrological language. It may be that there are purposes for this kind of talk which I have not been able to discern, and I'm more than willing to entertain the possibility that astrological talk serves therapeutic or even social ends of some significance perhaps. But as science, it is stupid. As religion, it is crazy.

Oftentimes in public matters, the question of what sort of semantic environment one is confronted with must be settled, as in the instance of Watergate. One might say that the whole issue of Watergate centered around the question, How shall we talk to each other about the events that took place? In other words, into what semantic environment should we place matters? Mr. Nixon, Mr. Ehrlichman, and others of their team insisted on using the language of patriotism and, by doing so, tried to give a particular direction to our attitudes toward their motives. They did what they did, they said, to protect national security, to protect the CIA, to prevent political disruptions, and so on. This is the semantic environment from which Mr. Nixon produced the memorable remark that members of his campaign organization were guilty merely of an "excess of zeal." We may call a patriot "overzealous," but we would not use that term for a thief who, let us say, steals more than he needs to. Of course, that was exactly the point made by Senators Ervin, Baker, and Weicker, who insisted on using the language of law, and by so doing were attempting to rule out of order any and all words that comprise the language of patriotism. Thus, the senators asked, Was perjury committed? Who bribed whom? Who was behind the break-in? And so on. You do not ask such questions about "patriots." You ask such questions about "crooks." What is the difference between a "patriot" and a "crook"? This is sometimes a difficult question to answer, but in Watergate the answer came easily. The tapes decided the issue. Not because Nixon used dirty words, which is certainly forgivable to patriots under stress, but because the tapes revealed that in the privacy of the Oval Office, Nixon and the other patriots used the language of law and crime to explain to themselves what they were doing. If you ask how money can be laundered and how much it will take to buy someone's silence, you are obviously speaking from a point of view which excludes patriotic sentiment.

In other words, the language of each social structure expresses human purpose through its tone, its vocabulary, its point of view, its metaphors, its level of abstraction. Watergate was a clash of two different semantic environments, as was the case of Lieutenant Calley and, incidentally, that of Adolf Eichmann. The issue raised with both Calley and Eichmann was, Which semantic environment shall prevail—the military situation or the ethical situation? The phrase *obeying orders* and the phrase *individual responsibility* do not occupy the same semantic environment, and I doubt if they can ever be made to. Two semantic environments usually will not coexist healthfully in the same space-time. There are some, of course, that *can*, for a while, because they look something like each other, as, let us say, a policeman looks a little bit like a soldier. But if you will look carefully enough, you will see that each has its unique forms and its special jurisdiction and its particular functions. We must attend to these differences and respect them, for if we call upon the wrong one, our thoughts become addled and our purposes confounded. We begin to talk stupid or crazy.

Consider: A merchant, at Christmastime, places a sign

on the window of his shop. It reads: "Buy—for the sake of Christ." What's the problem? Christ, Himself, gave the answer: "Render unto Caesar the things which be Caesar's and unto God the things which be God's." In other words, there is nothing wrong with commerce. But there is a special language in which it must be conducted, and that language nowhere touches upon the language of religion. They are different spheres of human enterprise and motivation, and in mixing them, we weaken both.

A proposal is put forward by a feminist group, the purpose of which is to get husbands and wives to share equally in household chores. The proposal involves having each partner sign a contract which specifies who would do what and on which days. The question is, Can the language of law solve a problem of this sort? It is true enough that marriage itself is a legal contract, but its stipulations are invoked only at the point where the marriage is in the process of being dissolved. Can anyone plausibly imagine an overburdened wife, having failed to persuade her husband that she needs his help, pulling out a contract from the bureau drawer and insisting he live up to its terms, on pain of legal sanctions? This is not marriage; it is the end of marriage. The language of the law is a great and useful instrument, but it is designed for the use of strangers, not lovers.

Another example: In many communities around the country, the quality of education is being measured by the scores children achieve on standardized tests. Education thus falls under the jurisdiction of the language of statistics, and it is a fact that many schools are now designing their programs almost solely for the purpose of increasing their students' mean test scores. Here, it is slightly unfair for me to repeat the joke about the statistician who drowned while trying to wade across a river with an average depth of two feet. The fault is not with statisticians, whose special language is a remarkably useful instrument for uncovering abstract facts. The fault is with those educators who have fallen under its spell and have allowed their purposes to be subverted by the seductions of precise measurement.

What all these examples are leading to is the beginning outline of a standard for the judgment of talk. The argument goes like this: One of the fundamental principles of life is differentiation. It is differentiation—the contrasts between one thing and another—that produces the energy for growth and change. Where there is no differentiation—of purpose, structure, role, function— you have, in natural and social systems, entropy: decay, uselessness, and death. Differentiation among social systems is codified and preserved—indeed, made visible— through language. When language becomes undifferentiated, human situations disintegrate: Science becomes indistinguishable from religion, which becomes indistinguishable from commerce, which becomes indistinguishable from law, and so on. If each of them serves the same function, then none of them serves any function. When such a process is occurring, an appropriate word for it is *pollution*. And I am here using that word in almost the same sense as it is used in natural ecology. To pollute a river means to introduce into it elements that cannot be absorbed, elements that do not fit, elements that have no function in the life system of the river. And that is how you pollute a semantic environment. You introduce

[handwritten margin note: entropy ↓ chaos NOT emaciation or waste ↓? as in atrophy]

a language whose tone or point of view or vocabulary has no function in the meaning system of that environment. Of course, any environment, natural or semantic, can tolerate a certain amount of unassimilable matter, i.e., garbage. I do not wish to say that the opposite of a polluted semantic environment is a "pure" semantic environment, whatever such a phrase might mean. But if you go beyond a certain point in introducing elements that do not "belong," an environment becomes toxic. In the case of a semantic environment, it becomes useless for the expression of certain human relationships and purposes.

And so, we have in the concept of a semantic environment our first criterion for identifying stupid or crazy talk. Stupid talk is talk that does not know what environment it is in. It is talk that comes from a world of human activity other than that which the situation calls for. Crazy talk is talk that creates and sustains an irrational environment, a situation that is not called for at all. But that's just the beginning. The very beginning.

Purposes

If the purpose of every semantic environment were singular and unambiguous, then among the several benefits that would accrue to the world is that the book before you would be unnecessary. Of somewhat more importance is that the flow of stupid or crazy talk in our lives would be a well-channeled trickle instead of a torrent. And of still more importance is that life would be unbearably dull, resembling in its simplicity and clarity a society of horseshoe crabs.

Whatever impression I may recently have given—for example, in the last chapter—the fact is that every semantic environment is generated by and organized around not one purpose but several. In fact, one of the principal reasons why people are forever quarreling about the quality and relevance of their remarks is that semantic environments are multipurposed. In approaching these purposes, we must be exceedingly cautious, for we are moving into a territory that has confounded many intellectual adventurers, some of whom found themselves in a swamp and have never been heard from again.

What *are* the purposes of such situations as go by the names of religion, war, politics, commerce, education, sports, science, law . . . ? For every purpose I will name, you will name two, and the list will grow endlessly— especially if we take recourse to the assumptions of psychoanalysis. Why do we have wars? I have been told that wars are contrived so that old men, who do not have to fight them, can have access to young women. Politics, I have read recently, is only an outlet for the male bonding instinct. And education? To keep children off the labor market. Religion, of course, is the opiate of the people.

Where do we go from here? It's a puzzlement. And yet, the question must be addressed. If we cannot get at the purposes of a human situation, in some reasonable way, then we cannot make any useful qualitative statements about language. Therefore, some attempt must be made to clarify the issue, and in the next several pages I will try it, although not by taking the hard route. I shall, so to speak, fly over the swamp rather than wade into it.

I must tell you then that I will not try here to catalogue the purposes of particular semantic environments. Instead, I want to offer a set of principles and questions that can be used in sorting out the complexities and confusions of purpose. As you have gathered by now, I am trying to establish, preeminently, that there can be no meaningful concept of either "good" or "bad" language without respect to purpose. If it seems to you that I have already said this several times (most recently, about five sentences back), I plead guilty with an explanation. I labor the point because most books on language neglect it entirely or at least try to hide it. From Fowler to Orwell to Korzybski to Chase to Edwin Newman—the list is legion—standards, rules, and guidelines for "good" talk have been put forward as if they applied to all human situations, when, in fact, they apply to very few. "Anything that depersonalizes is an enemy of language," Newman writes in his popular book, *Strictly Speaking*. But this is nonsense. The language of science depersonalizes, and that is exactly what it needs to do in order to serve its purpose. The First Law of Thermodynamics, for example, applies to Edwin Newman only in the most abstract way. It dehumanizes him, but it is not therefore an enemy of anything. Korzybski, on the other hand, insisted that the language of science alone is the language of sanity. But sanity has many more forms of expression than can be encompassed in a single semantic environment. The language of prayer is not scientific, but only in the most impoverished conception of the human enterprise can it be called insane.

The line I am taking here is that while the language of science, for example, has purposes that go far beyond making rockets or biochemical discoveries, such purposes can in no sense be regarded as the highest goal of human wisdom. Objective, detached, unambiguous, public, and tentative language is "good" in the context of the situation called science. But such language is decidedly "bad" in a number of other situations whose purposes differ from those of science—for example, in the process of love-making or praying, where language, in order to be "good," must be emotional, private, subjective, and categorical.

"Good" talk, I will continue to insist throughout, is talk that does what it's supposed to do in a particular situation, assuming that the purpose of that situation is to serve rational and humane ends. "Bad" talk is talk that doesn't. When I accuse astrologers of crazy talk, my assertion is based on my answers to a series of questions, including What are the purposes of religious language? and, To what extent does this language contradict such purposes? My answers are, of course, debatable, but they proceed from an assessment of specific purposes and not from some generalized notion of what is or is not an "enemy of language." Language, in fact, has no "enemies." (Or friends, for that matter.) But we might say that language can be one's "enemy" if one tries to achieve purposes with words that are not designed to serve them.

Any book about language is, therefore, a book about human purposes. And because human purposes are so difficult to understand and articulate, the most helpful thing I can do is to develop some distinctions.

The first is simple enough. There is a difference between the purposes of any individuals in a social situation and the purposes of the situation itself. Every semantic environment is an abstraction—an idea, if you will—and, therefore, has an existence independent of the individuals who make use of it. In other words, a semantic environment does not wholly belong to individuals. It is a product of our collective imagination; it belongs largely to tradition, and it is fashioned from a society's experience of what is useful conduct. Here is a simple example from a common enough social semantic environment: Two people who are acquainted with each other pass on the street. The first says, "Hi, howyabin?" The second says, "Fine. Yourself?" The first: "Pretty good. See you around." The second: "Right. See ya." Now, if I tell you that these two people dislike each other intensely, you will begin to see what I mean. It is not what *they* wish to say that matters. It is what the *situation* wishes them to say. A million times before, on a million different streets, a million different people have had a roughly similar conversation. Who knows when and where this tradition started? We can assume only that its basic purpose is to maintain a minimum level of civility—indeed, *require* a minimum level of civility— especially when individuals may be inclined to take the conversation in a more disagreeable direction.

Moreover, it would be shallow to call this situation a "mere" convention. Its rules are a distillation of countless concrete transactions of the past, and the sturdiness of its purpose is shown by the infrequency of the occasions on which an individual will defy its constraints. And what do we normally say when someone does? Example: First person: "Hi, howyabin?" Second person: "It's none of your goddam business, you hypocrite!" The first person now thinks of the second person that there is something "wrong" with him. Why? Because, in part, what we *mean* by "something wrong" is that someone has failed to grasp the purpose of a semantic environment, has confused his own requirements with those of the situation.

With characteristic insight, Charles Schulz has drawn

a well-known "Peanuts" cartoon which gets to the heart of the matter. Charlie Brown is screaming at Lucy because she has made a bonehead play in their baseball game. "You threw to the wrong base again!" he bawls. "There were runners on first and second, and you threw the ball to first! In a situation like that, you always throw to third or home!" Lucy considers his advice for a moment and then boldly replies, "You're destroying my creativity!!" Maybe so. But whatever purposes are served through such creativity, they appear to work against the purposes of baseball. If you are in a baseball game, or any other systematized event, what *you* want must be expressed through what the situation demands. This is what is meant by social order, without which communication is quite impossible. And so Lucy will have to negotiate between her purposes and the game's—which is what we all must do most of the time in each of the semantic environments we are in. And when we fail to do so, someone is going to think that we are talking either stupid or crazy, or maybe a little of both. But sometimes it gets awfully complicated, and who is talking stupid or crazy and who isn't is not so easy to say.

In October 1973, Doreen Rappaport and her fiancé went to City Hall in New York City to get a marriage license. There, they saw a sign which read:

> Women are not permitted to wear slacks.
> Men must wear a tie and a jacket.
> One or more rings must be exchanged.

Ms. Rappaport was outraged on two counts. She believed these regulations to be a violation of her civil rights. And they would clearly prevent her from wearing a green velvet pants suit which she had purchased in Paris specifically for the marriage ceremony. Eventually, she instigated a lawsuit charging that the regulation banning slacks for brides and requiring coats and ties for bridegrooms was unconstitutional. Her anger was particularly directed at a man named Herman Katz, who was, at the time, the City Clerk and was responsible for setting up the regulations and enforcing them. Here are some of the things Mr. Katz had to say in his defense: "The law prescribes the 'solemnization' of marriages, and that word permits me to require appropriate dress.... The question is whether [the regulation] is reasonable, and I don't believe I'm being arbitrary.... Once I allow pants, everything is permissible. They could come in here with overalls. We've had hippies come in wearing practically nothing at all.... Marriage is a very dignified matter. We are not dispensing supermarket produce, where you walk in not mattering how you're dressed, plunk down five dollars, and pick up what you came for."

To this definition of the situation, Ms. Rappaport contrasted hers: "Since a wedding is such a personal event, tastes and attitudes surrounding it considerably vary from person to person. I feel that an adult has the right to make his/her decisions as to what clothing or jewelry is suitable for this occasion." She also said, "I don't think most people in the twentieth century agree with Herman Katz."

This little dispute is intriguing, I think, because it is an example of a disagreement over the purposes of a particular social structure and, of course, the rules which best express those purposes. It is too early in this book to alienate any portion of my readers (the astrologers are gone by now, I'm sure) by applying such a term as "stupid talk" to either Ms. Rappaport's or Mr. Katz's comments. Nor do I think it much warranted. In fact, I will confess that, for all his Victorian intransigence, Mr. Katz seems to have at least one good argument in his favor. This is that Ms. Rappaport could not possibly be more wrong in saying that a wedding is a personal event. If it were, then how would Mr. Katz get into the act in the first place? Why would Ms. Rappaport and her fiancé seek a license? Why would they have to repeat certain words in a precise way before a public official? The answer, of course, is that marriage is not only *not* a personal event (although one's *feelings* about it might be); it is one of the most public rituals we have. Ms. Rappaport and her fiancé could choose to live together without the sanction of the state. But they have chosen instead to "go public." That is what a wedding is.

The question as to whether this is a personal or a public event, then, would appear to veer in Mr. Katz's favor. And he tries to codify this judgment by relying on what he construes to be traditional practice. He thinks he lives in a society in which most people believe a wedding, as ritual confirmation of the society's values, is made solemn by a dress and a coat and tie. Ms. Rappaport says no, and heaps down upon him the hypothetical consensus of all people who live in the twentieth century, most of whom, she says, disagree with poor old Herman Katz. Well, I don't know about that and, in fact, find it difficult to imagine the sources from which she draws her evidence. I am inclined to think that if a vote were taken on the matter, Mr. Katz would win big in New York and

New Jersey, where I have attended many weddings and have not yet seen a bride in a pants suit. But I cannot speak about Pakistan or Cambodia or, for that matter, Connecticut.

In any event, before going on to other matters, I want to remind you that the example is put forward to show how differing perceptions of the purposes of a semantic environment will lead to differing judgments about the structure of its rules. To Mr. Katz, the purpose of the situation is to reaffirm cultural values through solemn public ritual; its rules, therefore, call for a high degree of uniformity and respect for tradition and a corresponding degree of suppression of individual taste or preference. To Ms. Rappaport, the purpose of the situation is to give personal expression to one's feelings of love and devotion; therefore, it ought not to have any hard and fast rules and certainly should allow for the widest possible expression of individual style. Mr. Katz is Charlie Brown saying you're supposed to throw the ball to third. Ms. Rappaport is Lucy saying you're destroying my creativity.

It remains for me to say of such disagreements over purpose—and this one in particular—that they are rarely amenable to empirical solution; with a few exceptions, there is no way to test one view against another. For Mr. Katz and Ms. Rappaport are not arguing over what the purposes of a wedding *are*; they are arguing over what the purposes of a wedding *should be*. And where you stand on such matters depends largely on your values, on your assessment of what is to be gained and what is to be lost.

Another source of conflict over purposes derives from

the fact that frequently there is a difference between the avowed purposes of a semantic environment and the purposes that may be inferred from the way in which the environment is structured. In other words, *hypothetical* (or stated) purposes may contrast sharply with *actual* (or achieved) purposes, and when people are unaware of this difference, the amount of stupid talk generated can be alarming. A school teacher I know told me once —sincerely, I believe—that the main purpose of his lessons was to help youngsters become independent, analytical thinkers who know how to ask well-formed and relevant questions. But when I had the opportunity to observe his class in action, it was immediately obvious that its actualized purpose was something else. The teacher did all the question-asking and, in fact, most of the answer-giving. The situation was arranged so that the highest possible value was placed on conformity, if not obedience. Here, I am not contending that conformity and obedience are in any sense worse purposes than diversity and independence. I am only saying that sometimes the latter purposes are avowed, but the former are achieved. Or vice versa. There is, in short, a difference between what people say they want to do or ought to do and what they are actually doing.

Consider, for instance, the following problem which surfaced in 1975 during Congressional debates over gun control. Congressman Robert Sikes of Florida spoke against gun control. "Firearms," he said, "are used by American citizens to protect their lives, families, and property. The need to possess them for self-defense today is as great, if not greater, than in earlier periods of our nation's history." Congressman Jonathan Bingham of the Bronx not only disagreed, he proposed legislation to restrict the manufacture of handguns. He then proceeded to say the following: "I think we are literally out of our minds to allow 2.5 million new weapons to be manufactured each year for the sole purpose of killing people."

Assuming that Congressman Bingham knows the conventional meaning of the word *literally*, it would appear that he thinks Congressman Sikes not only talks a little crazy but *is* crazy and perhaps ought to be institutionalized (in some place other than Congress). But, of course, Bingham probably doesn't mean *literally* to be taken literally, which is a common enough mistake and, in any case, beside the point. The point is that both congressmen agree, here, that one of the important purposes of government is to protect its citizens against violence. Their argument is not at the abstract level of avowed purpose. Both of them could state that purpose in an Independence Day speech with roughly the same conviction. Where they disagree—and where the trouble starts—is over the concrete question, What sort of situation would afford the most protection for citizens?

Sikes believes that law-abiding citizens are protected best in a society which makes handguns easily available to all. Bingham believes that such protection is best achieved in a society which tightly controls the availability of weapons. This dispute is, to a large extent, an empirical issue. If Bingham's law is tried, we can find out through experience whether he is right or wrong.

Of course, experience is often the definitive method by which we can distinguish between avowed and actualized purposes. Without recourse to "reality testing," we cannot know if the purposes for which we have been organized, in any situation, are in fact being achieved. Coaches tell us that the purpose of athletics is to help people develop character and learn the value of sportsmanship. But witnessing even one Little League game tells you that its purpose is something else. Scientists tell us that one of the purposes of science is to help people develop an open mind and a wide, humane perspective. But as experience has shown, scientists are awfully quick to sell their services to the state, at the cost of closing their minds and limiting their perspectives.

It so happens that I think gun control is an excellent idea. But, as with Rappaport and Katz, I will let Sikes and Bingham shoot it out without my interference. My main purpose in using this example is to show that people can agree at one level of purpose but collide—and bitterly—when matters are removed to a more concrete level.

Another source of conflict—somewhat similar to the one just described—derives from the fact that the purpose served by a semantic environment is sometimes contradicted by the purposes of some subsystem which belongs to it. For example, as I argued earlier, religion has as its overriding purpose the creation of a sense of oneness, stressing the connectedness of all people. No major existing religion envisions God as a regional potentate. And yet there is no shortage of examples of religious practices, rituals, and institutions motivated by the idea that people are morally different, that some will have access to eternity and some will not. All religious conflict stems from the idea of exclusiveness, while, paradoxically, all true religious sentiment promotes the idea of inclusiveness.

The difference between the purposes of subsystems and the purposes of suprasystems continuously creates paradoxes—sometimes unresolvable ones. For example, consider the following tragic story, recounted in Gore Vidal's *Esquire* article "Passage to Egypt":

Ahmed told me another story of military service, involving friends. "Each year in the army they have these maneuvers," he said. "So these friends of mine are in maneuvers with guns in the desert and they have orders: shoot to kill. Now one of them was Ibrahim, my friend. Ibrahim goes to this outpost in the dark. They make him stop and ask him for the password. But he has forgotten the password. So they say, 'He must be the enemy.'"

I asked if this took place in wartime. "No, no, maneuvers. My friend Ibrahim say, 'Look, I forget. I did know but now I forget the password but you know me, anyway, you know it's Ibrahim.' And he's right; they do know it was Ibrahim.... But since he cannot say the password they shot him."

"Shot him? Dead?"

"Dead," said my host, with melancholy satisfaction. "Oh, they were sorry, very sorry, because they knew it was Ibrahim, but you see, he did not know the password, and while he was dying in the tent they took him to, he said it was all right. They were right to kill him."

Ibrahim is dead, killed by his friends. To serve what purpose? Assuming that, from the largest perspective, the aim of the Egyptian army is to protect Egyptians from Israelis, by what reasoning can everyone, including the victim, acquiesce in the shooting of one of their own, during peacetime maneuvers, for nothing worse than forgetting a password? The answer is that, at certain levels, military organizations have purposes all their own that do not always match the reasons why an army is formed in the first place. The purpose of these maneuvers, it would appear, was not to protect Egyptians from Israelis but simply to compel obedience from the troops. You might argue, of course, that extracting blind obedience from soldiers is a first step toward achieving an effective army. But most generals, I think, would disagree. They are apt to become very irritable when their own men deplete the size of their army, especially in peacetime. As a rule, generals want obedience and judgment together, and if I am wrong about Egyptian generals, perhaps we have one possible explanation as to why they have made so little headway against the Israelis in the past.

In any event, we have here a case where the basic purpose of the larger system (to defeat other armies) is contradicted by the basic purpose of a subsystem (to achieve blind obedience), and such contradictions are frequently at the core of stupid or crazy talk. Incidentally, this particular case demonstrates many interesting causes of crazy talk, among which is the widely popular, and almost always disastrous, *identification reaction*—that is, thinking by definition. If you do not know the password, you are, by definition, the enemy. And if you are the enemy, you must, by definition, be killed. This is a form of craziness that occurs in many different semantic environments, and it invariably provokes intriguing questions. For example, suppose one of the soldiers in camp

—let us say, someone about to go to sleep—suddenly
realizes he has forgotten the password. By definition, he
is now the enemy. Should he shoot himself? After all,
what can be more dangerous than to have the enemy
sleeping among you? Well, if there is an Egyptian general anywhere who would say, "Yes, he should," then we
know for sure why they have been losing to the Israelis.

When you are in a situation in which communication
has broken down, in which there is the strongest impulse
to say that someone is talking stupid or crazy, even if it's
yourself, you have then three questions to help you uncover the problem: Do the purposes of the situation
contradict the purposes of individuals functioning within
it? Do the avowed purposes contradict those that can be
inferred from the way events are actually going? Are
there contradictions in the purposes of different levels
and subsystems of the environment? If we add to these
the questions developed in the chapter "The Semantic
Environment"—Are there two different semantic environments competing for control of the situation? and Are
they contradictory in their purposes?—we will have covered some of the important sources of conflict concerning
purpose.

Conflict, of course, is the key word here. Where there
is no perceived conflict in purposes, there is usually no
awareness of a problem. To Ibrahim's friends and to
Ibrahim himself, for example, no question arose, so far
as we know, about stupidity or craziness. Killers and
victim alike shared the same assumptions about the purposes of their environment. It is only when someone
looks at the situation from a different set of assumptions
that a problem arises. We must keep in mind that stupid

talk and crazy talk are, first and foremost, problems. As I have said previously, they are not facts, like whether it snowed last Tuesday or not. They are products of a conflict between two different assessments of a situation.

Relationships

It's been a bad century for rules. Or so it would seem, as everywhere political, religious, economic, and social arrangements have been found obsolete and rudely overthrown. But it is an illusion, this disdain for rules. As soon as one set of them is cast out, another is quickly put in its place. The anthropologists tell us that humanity is the tool-making species. No doubt. But humanity is also the rule-making species. Put two people together with a common purpose, and in two minutes they will turn themselves into an organization. Then, they will produce a rule book. And soon after, a ritual or two to seal their bond.

The scientific way to explain this instinct—for example, according to the anthropologist Edward Hall—is that man has a biological need to organize frames of reference in order to minimize his fear of isolation. An artistic way to put it—for example, according to the cartoonist Shel Silverstein—is to draw a picture which shows two emaciated men at the bottom of a hundred-foot pit. The walls of the pit are made of smooth granite and are unscalable. Even a bird could not get out of the pit, because it is covered over with an impenetrable steel plate. Moreover, both men are chained to a wall, held fast by manacles which bind their arms, legs, and torsos. One of them now turns to the other and, with an indomitable light shining from his eyes, announces, "Now, here's my plan. . . ."

This is as good a metaphor of humanity as any I know, for it conveys not only the desperation and absurdity of the human condition but our unquenchable belief in the efficacy of order as a means of salvation. There is no such thing as an unstructured human situation. Unless it be a madhouse. Indeed, we use the term *madhouse* to describe a situation whose structure we cannot discern. And the essence of structure is, of course, rules. There are rules for street talk, rules for church talk, rules for courtroom talk, classroom talk, conference-room talk, and even concentration-camp talk. Rules for any human encounter with a past and a future; in other words, for every semantic environment. It is necessary, then, to identify and elaborate on the main categories into which the rules of talk fall. These may be placed under two large headings: relationship and content. I will deal here with some of the rules which govern relationship, and in the next chapter with those of content.

By relationship, I am referring to the rules that define the emotional context of a semantic environment, the rules that form the container in which the content of our talk is presented. Suppose, for example, you were observing some complex human transaction in which the language being used, but only the language, was completely unknown to you. Or, even better, suppose you were watching an event on television but with the sound turned off. Would you be able to make some sense of what you were seeing? Of course. You would, for example, probably be able to guess what the general purpose of the event is. And you might be able to tell who is running things, and who isn't. You might also know when the event has been interrupted, and certainly when it has been concluded; that is, what are its time and space boundaries. You would know these things, and more, because all talk has a frame in which it occurs, and the construction and appearance of each frame are governed by certain conditions. The first of these is what may be called tone, and I am using the word here to include both atmosphere and attitude. By atmosphere, I mean the ambience and texture of a semantic environment. This is something over which an individual rarely has any control. When you walk into a church or a ball park or a hospital or the stock exchange, you become aware at once of a particular coloration to the place and to the events that are occurring there. This is expressed in many ways, among which may be the level of noise, the spatial boundaries, the dress worn, the arrangement of furniture, the pace of people's movements, the types of side activities going on, etc. In this, I am saying nothing astonishing. You do not need to be told that hot dogs aren't sold in churches, and that if they were you would feel quite different about the meaning of what everyone is supposed to do there. However, it is not unusual, I might point out, to find people who are not especially sensitive to the atmosphere of an environment, and in such cases, their behavior is often thought to suggest some sort of stupidity, unless they can demonstrate that the environment in question is totally unfamiliar to them. I witnessed recently a striking and barely believable example of such behavior at a wedding ceremony. One of the guests said loud enough for those on my side of the chapel to hear, "Think it through, Jerry," just at the point where the rabbi had asked Jerry if he took this woman to be his lawful wedded wife, according to (no less) the laws of Moses and Israel. So far as I could tell, the wedding guest was not drunk or embittered. He merely mistook the synagogue for Shea Stadium, which, where I come from, usually happens the other way around.

It is probably worth noting that errors in interpreting the atmosphere of an environment are exceedingly frequent when people are in foreign countries. And if I am not mistaken, the term *culture shock* refers to the disorientation one may experience from a repeated inability to interpret the signs and symbols of atmosphere. Even if one has some familiarity with the language, the simplest semantic environments in a foreign country—for example, asking directions or checking into a hotel—can be surrounded by uncertainty and a sense that you have somehow missed the point. I will go so far as to say that even the peculiar (to Americans) color of foreign currency contributes to a confused sense of the atmosphere of certain situations. Personally, I have always found it difficult to believe that red paper bills have any utility whatsoever outside of a Monopoly game. As a consequence, I experience a sense of giddy delight in giving such bills to solemn foreigners, who apparently believe that they are getting something of value. The technical name for this belief of mine is stupidity.

A second element of tone includes all of the devices by which individuals show what their particular attitudes are toward the environment itself. I am talking here about such things as intonation, forms of address, nonverbal gestures, grunts, groans, sighs, pauses—everything that indicates our enthusiasm or reverence or defiance or indifference toward the situation we are in. Naturally, this is something over which individuals have considerable control, and most people work exceedingly hard and carefully to match their attitudes with the atmosphere. Some, of course, work just as hard and carefully to do the opposite. This may take the form of giggling at a funeral, being morbid at a going-away party, wearing dungarees and a sweat shirt to an investiture, or yawning, grunting, and groaning at faculty meetings (which is my particular specialty). You have doubtless been in situations where people who have the emotional and intellectual resources to match attitude with atmosphere have chosen, out of precise conviction, to express their contempt for a situation by a bizarre breach in attitude. Such behavior, in its extreme forms, is often thought to suggest some sort of craziness, if for no other reason than that it speaks of great discontent with the social order and one's place in it.

Now, it is very difficult to say exactly what are the "right" rules for the matching of attitude and atmosphere in each semantic environment. Every individual who is doing the "right" thing will do it in a unique way, and these differences in performance are, I believe, what we usually mean by the word style, style being individual variations on a general theme which is composed, so to speak, by the purposes of the environment. However, it is generally not difficult to know when someone is playing a different tune altogether. As with so many other things, we become conscious of attitude when its rules are being breached. It would take a lifetime of scholarly work, such as Erving Goffman has done, to catalogue the ways in which the harmony of a semantic environment may be interrupted and normal relationships wrecked. I will not attempt even a summary. I wish, however, to drive home one point about attitude which is not often discussed and which bears heavily on any attempt to define stupid or crazy talk. I am referring to the ways in which people learn about it. So far as I can tell, we learn the rules of attitude informally. I should even say haphazardly. In any case, there is very little explicit instruction given in the rules of attitude either in the home or in school—or anywhere else, for that matter. People are expected to learn the rules, but are not taught them systematically except, of course, by episodic "don'ts": "Ladies don't sit that way," "You must wait your turn to speak," "You're making too much noise," etc. There are, of course, books, like those on etiquette or, recently, on body language, which try to give advice on such matters, but they are invariably too specific to be much help in understanding the cultural meaning of attitude. They tell you, just as your parents and teachers did, what not to do in concrete situations. In this way, we may learn how to follow the rules, but we are not usually made conscious of the questions to which our attitudes, e.g., our manners, are the answers. These questions have to do with our opinions of ourselves and of the social structure we must enter, and, ultimately, of the advantages (or disadvantages) we see in becoming integrated into our culture. It has been said before, but is worth repeating, that good manners or bad are the most direct expression of our political philosophy. *Political philosophy* means here our fundamental ideas about the obligations people have toward each other and toward the situations our culture has contrived for us. What we think about the Middle East or apartheid is flimsy stuff compared to the ways in which we manage our attitudes toward different semantic environments. Our attitudes, insofar as we consciously direct them, are our public ballots on the purposes of different social arrangements. We vote ourselves in or out by matching or mismatching attitude with atmosphere.

In every situation, there is also a pecking order which tells us who talks when and to whom and, especially, in what sort of way. This pecking order may be called the role-structure of the environment, and one elementary distinction ought to be made at once: there are semantic environments whose role-structure is more or less fixed, and there are others whose role-structure is quite fluid. In the first instance, individuals have little choice but to assume their assigned places. To do otherwise is to wreck the environment altogether. In a classroom, for example, students are not permitted to go to the bathroom unless given permission, will not (unless given permission) address the teacher by his or her first name, and will not even go to the chalkboard without specific approval to do so. When students do not follow these rules, teachers call it chaos. In church, you do not argue with the minister's sermon, nor do you give one of your own, unless specifically asked. To assume a new role for yourself in situations where your role has been rigidly defined is an act of sabotage.

There are, however, semantic environments in which the role-structure is quite fluid, which simply means that the rules about who may peck whom, and how, are not so well-established that individuals cannot alter them to suit their needs and the strengths of their personalities. A first date between two people or a community meeting of some kind might be good examples. But whether fixed or fluid, a role-structure is always present, and ignorance of it is invariably dangerous.

Let us suppose, for example, a man has been called for an audit by the IRS. Unless he is among the 12 or 13 Americans who have filed an unimpeachable tax return, he will naturally be one-down in the situation, a "child" to the government agent's "adult." In fact, even if he *has* filed such a return, he will be in virtually the same position, since it is the government, not the taxpayer, who defines what "unimpeachable" means. Therefore, if his wits have not flown out the window, everything he does and says in his interview will try to convey that if his return is not absolutely legitimate, he is. This role will be executed in much the same way as one makes known more general attitudes toward the situation— through a deferential manner of sitting, a formal mode of address, a proper waiting for one's turn to speak, and so on. There are as many effective ways by which this role can be expressed as there are styles of being a child. As long as our taxpayer's role is appropriate, he and the examiner can get to the substance of the issue fairly efficiently. A noticeable problem arises, however, when he conveys a different definition of the role-structure of the situation; for example, that the examiner is the child and he the parent, or, to change the metaphor, that the examiner is on trial and he is the prosecutor. What happens then is that his tax return becomes a secondary issue, and the integrity of the role-structure becomes paramount. Everything goes on hold until the rules get straightened out. It is as if the words people exchange are the numbers in an arithmetic problem, whereas the role-structure is the arithmetical sign—plus or minus—which tells you how the numbers are to be handled. Naturally, you don't get very far until it is decided which it will be, adding or subtracting.

There are no rules, I have found, to which people are more sensitive than those of role-structure. Nor to which they will take greater offense when a breach occurs. Pity the poor child who intervenes when his parents are having an argument. Not only will the one whose cause he rejects turn on him, but so will the one whose cause he espouses. Why? Because the substance of the argument—that is, its content—is of little importance compared to the maintenance of the role-structure of the environment. To challenge that structure is to threaten not only the authority but the rationality of everyone in it.

Of course, if such a challenge arises through one's ignorance of the rules, there is frequently an ample margin of tolerance for the breach. But if the challenge is motivated by defiance, then reprisals—you can be sure of it—are always quick and decisive. I remember, with great clarity, an incident, bearing on this point, that occurred during my morbid career in the U.S. Army. While I was stationed at Fort Dix, my outfit was promised a weekend pass. One of our men was an enthusiastic nine-teen-year-old romantic from Winston-Salem, North Carolina, who in anticipation of the weekend had arranged for his seventeen-year-old sweetheart to meet him in Trenton, where the two of them could frolic in the New Jersey sun for two days. (In those days, the sun still shone in Trenton.) But on Saturday morning—at the last minute, so to speak—someone must have been disobedient, and in retribution, all passes were canceled, and every man was confined to the barracks. The young man was distraught and pleaded with our lieutenant to allow him to go to Trenton anyway, or, failing that, at least to allow him to telephone the hotel where his girlfriend was to stay. To these pleas, the lieutenant turned two deaf ears, and as he started to leave the barracks, was presented with an unexpected dilemma. "I'll tell you what," said the young private, "why don't we let the men in the barracks vote on it, and I'll go along with whatever they say." For a moment, the lieutenant did not react, as he tried to decide if this proposal was a consequence of naïveté, in which case a benign smile would have done nicely as an answer, or impudence, in which case there were some well-known military traditions to cover the matter. Well, he was a lieutenant and not a semanticist, and probably felt strained at dwelling upon such distinctions. In any case, he did not pause long before adding another punishment to the one already given, on the grounds that the young private was making a mockery of the U.S. Army. Which, of course, in his innocence or desperation, he was.

I hope it is clear that in this instance the problem did not arise from a failure on the private's part to use the proper "tone of voice." He was polite enough, and his challenge to the situation did not originate in a contemptuous manner of speaking. The issue was his failure to grasp or accept the rules for decision-making in the Army, which rules have never included holding plebiscites. It is all a matter of seeing the parameters of one's jurisdiction—what you are allowed to say, as well as how you are allowed to say it. The private's remark is simply the equivalent of someone's failing to stand in a courtroom when the judge enters or of telling the government agent who is auditing your return that he does not know the tax regulations as well as you do, which may be true but is monstrously irrelevant.

There is one point about role-structure which requires some special illumination, because it has so much to do with stupid and crazy talk. I am referring to its highly conservative nature. Role-structures are exceedingly resistant to change, partly because people tend to be unaware of them and partly because they give an essential stability to situations. There is an old joke, best told with a slight Jewish accent, about a jury which has been out for two days after having listened to arguments in a divorce case. When the jury returns to court, the judge asks what their decision is. "Well, I'll tell you, Your Honor," says the foreman, "we turned it over in our minds, and we've decided not to mix in." But, of course, juries *must* mix in. If they do not, the courtroom loses its point, and everyone in it loses his bearing. Teachers who have experimented with novel role-structures in the classroom can testify to the extreme reluctance of students to accept any arrangement where, for example, there is a redistribution of authority. Students will accept a new content—let us say, the study of archeology instead of mathematics—but what is almost unbearable is a situation where the teacher is not the teacher and the student not the student. It is probably an exaggeration to say that people come to love the role-structure of situations. But they surely depend on it in the most fundamental way, and with good reason. Our world falls apart, even if only for a while, when we cannot predict how each of us will behave. This is true not only for solemn semantic environments such as courtrooms, schools, and board rooms, but for any environment. Consider, for example, a baseball game. You do not get a baseball game simply by gathering together some men and a bat and a ball. You get a baseball game when the men agree to distribute themselves in a certain way and follow specific rules. Everyone has to play a predictable role, or you have no game. If the pitcher declines to throw to the catcher because he has had an argument with him, you do not have a baseball game with a spiteful pitcher—you have no baseball game. If the umpire refuses to make decisions on balls and strikes because he doesn't want to antagonize anyone, you do not have a baseball game with an amiable umpire. Again: no game. Now, it is entirely possible to design something resembling a baseball game in which there are no umpires, in which the players vote on balls and strikes, and in which the third baseman may, whenever the impulse moves him, take a turn at bat (the Designated Third Baseman?). But that would be another game, and it would be difficult to get very many people to take it seriously. A baseball game is, in fact, almost nothing but a role-structure, its "content" being wholly expressed in the sentence The Pirates 4 and the Cubs 2. One might even say that the principal cultural value of baseball and other games is that they stress the importance of orderly role-structuring as a means of cooperative action.

The conservative nature of the role-structure of semantic environments explains why in countries where major political revolutions have occurred, there is rarely any fundamental change in the structure of authority. We may get new *names* for old roles—for example, premier instead of czar—but the relationship between ruler and ruled stays exactly the same. The content of a situation, as Marshall McLuhan once said, may be likened to the bone a thief throws to the watchdog while he peacefully makes off with the goods. Like the dog, we are apt to busy ourselves with the bone and neglect to see what is really happening. Writers like George Orwell and Arthur Koestler, who saw, for example, that the role-structure of the political environment in Russia was the same after the Revolution as before, were thought by many in the intellectual community to be reactionary spoilsports. Those who see the same in China today get the same response.

From one point of view, the tendency of semantic environments to maintain their role-structure is quite important, since it obviously provides us with a basis for predictable continuity in life. But from another point of view, it can be seen as a source of the most extreme depravity. A few years ago, Professor Stanley Milgram conducted a now controversial experiment which bears directly on this point. He arranged a situation in which people believed they were to participate in a psychological experiment concerning memory and learning. They

were put in a laboratory setting in which they were required to administer electric shocks to a person whose
capacity to remember certain words was allegedly being
measured. Actually, this person was an accomplice of
Milgram's, was not actually wired to receive any shocks,
and had no intention of remembering anything; thus, requiring the true subjects of the experiment to administer
what they believed to be increasingly severe shocks. Milgram, of course, was interested in finding out how far
people will go in inflicting pain on another human being
for no other reason than that they were instructed to do
so by "scientists" within the context of an "experiment."
What he found out got him into an awful lot of trouble
—a case of damning the messenger because of the un-
pleasantness of the message. Roughly 60 percent of the
subjects were fully obedient; that is, on being told to administer the "shocks," they did so and, in some cases,
gave "shocks" of such severity that they would have
badly injured the "victim" had the situation been real.
Although many of these people suffered emotional dis-
tress later, realizing what they had done, Milgram was
able to conclude that Hannah Arendt's conception of the
banality of evil is more than a metaphor. "The ordinary
person," Milgram wrote, "who shocked the victim did so
out of a sense of obligation—a conception of his duties
as a subject—and not from any peculiarly aggressive
tendencies. . . . Ordinary people, simply doing their jobs,
and without any particular hostility on their part, can
become agents in a terrible destructive process." At the
end of his study, he remarks that "where legitimate authority is the source of action, *relationship overwhelms
content* [his italics]. That is what is meant by the impor-

tance of social structure, and that is what is demonstrated in the present experiment." What the italicized words mean is that what you ask people to do is not as important as the "role" which asks them to do it. Another way of saying this is that people will do almost anything to keep a role-structure intact. (At least, a majority of people will.) But this is not to say that because their behavior appears to be "normal," it is not also crazy. I should say that in one sense Milgram's subjects were crazier than the Egyptian soldiers who killed Ibrahim. The soldiers could justify their actions on the grounds that if they had not shot Ibrahim, they, in turn, might have been shot. But what drove Milgram's subjects to such cruelty? A fear of not playing their parts. A failure to ask, Why am I listening to this man? One may also ask, of course, what drove Milgram to inflict such cruelty on his "subjects." The answer, no doubt, would be much the same: a fear of not playing his part as a "productive scientist," a failure to ask, What are the limits of the semantic environment of science?

Of course, there are always some people who *will* ask such questions, who will pay attention to the consequences of their roles, and who will not, therefore, easily say or do crazy things. They would not perform every role they were assigned simply because their failure to do so would jeopardize the structure of the environment. There are questions to ask and decisions to be made. And there are environments that ought not to be perpetuated.

But we would be foolish, I think, to underestimate the power that the rules of ordering possess over our behavior. The reason is, if I may return to an earlier metaphor, that these rules are the soil, sun, air, and water of a semantic environment. If communication is to happen, these elements must be present in a predictable pattern to support the life of the plant. As for the plant itself, that is the subject to which we must now turn.

Content

In Woody Allen's book *Getting Even*, he gives us a rundown on some of the key men in the Mafia, one of whom is named Albert (The Logical Positivist) Carillo. What makes this funny, of course, is Woody's mixing of two worlds of discourse which may be in the same universe but are light-years away from each other. The joke is roughly the same (but not as funny) as the one we encounter in the Elizabeth Barrett Browning poem which she begins with "How do I love thee?" and then, her pocket calculator at the ready, proceeds to, "Let me count the ways." Perhaps the poem was intended to be read at a convention of public accountants.

Every semantic environment is recognizable not only by its tone and role-structure, but by the words it uses and the special ways in which it uses them. My purpose here is to indicate some of the important rules which define the content of semantic environments.

The first of these is that every semantic environment

has a technical vocabulary. In politics, law, religion, war, commerce, science, sports—in whatever system of human enterprise we can isolate—there are certain words which form the core of the content of the subject. Some of these are so specialized or technical that they never appear in any semantic environment other than the one which has given them life and to which they, in turn, give life. For example, if the phrase *Planck's constant* comes out of someone's mouth—let us say, twice in the span of five minutes—we can be fairly sure that physics is the subject she's discussing. Or suppose you are in a restaurant and, over the hubbub, you become aware of a discussion at the next table. You miss most of what is being said, but you catch the phrases *rules of evidence, statute of limitations, hung jury,* and *civil tort.* You know, of course, that the subject is not quantum physics—which is fine, since lawyers don't know anything about that. What I am saying here is nothing more than that each semantic environment has a characteristic technical vocabulary which distinguishes it from any other.

But there is more to say about this than you might think. For example, contrary to what many people believe, the words which comprise a semantic environment are not so much *about* a subject as they *are* the subject itself. Subtract all the words that are used in discussing physics or law or theology, and you have just about subtracted the subject altogether. If there is nothing to talk *with*, there is nothing to talk *about*. Of course, you can invent new words to take the place of the old ones, but until you do so, you have a world of things, not meanings. In fact it is only a small exaggeration to say that all knowledge is language. History, for example, is not past events; it is a way of talking about past events. And astronomy is not stars and planets but a particular way of talking about them. The sentence "The moon is beautiful" is not astronomy. But the sentence "The moon influences the tides" is.

There is an old joke about a mother who is boasting to a neighbor of her son's academic achievements. To prove how smart he is, the mother calls him into the room and says, "Harold, say something in geometry for Mrs. Green." Now, the point of this joke is supposed to be that in thinking one can say something in geometry, the mother demonstrated her own ignorance, not her son's brilliance. But in fact there is no point to the joke, since Harold *could* say something in geometry, and quite easily. Like: "The whole is equal to the sum of its parts," which, incidentally, is a true statement in geometry but false just about everyplace else.

Words are not only tools to think with. They are, for all practical purposes, the content of our thoughts. As Ludwig (The Logical Positivist) Wittgenstein put it: Language is not only the vehicle of thought; it is also the driver. In putting forward this idea, I am not implying (nor did Wittgenstein) that the world consists only of words. I am saying, however, that what meanings we give to the world—what sense we make of things—derive from our power to name, to create vocabularies.

The process by which words and other symbols give shape and substance to our thoughts can be suggested by your trying to multiply 495 by 384. Except in this instance you must use only Roman numerals. I think you will find the operation quite impossible to do. Without access to the symbol o and a system of positional notation, the answer is literally inconceivable, i.e., you cannot think it. Perhaps more to the point: Try to describe to another person what goes on in the place we call *school* but without using such terms as school, teacher, student, principal, test, grades, subject, course, curriculum, syllabus, homework, or any of the more or less technical terms which comprise the vocabulary of that semantic environment. I do not say that it cannot be done, but my guess is that what you will end up describing will be barely recognizable as a "school." Perhaps it will sound like a prison or a hospital or a rehabilitation center. It depends. And it depends on what words you use in place of those you have given up.

One more example: Consider the two different vocabularies that are commonly used to describe drug use. One of them you will hear every fifteen minutes or so on television. "Mother!" shouts an irate young woman. "I can do it myself!" What's wrong with her? She is "upset," her "nerves are jangled," she's not "feeling well," she can't go on with her "work." The recommended solution is to take a drug—aspirin, Bufferin, tranquilizers, Nytol, etc. The language here is the language of illness and medical care, and on that account, I assume, the narcotics agents pay it no attention. But what the audience is being advised to take can also be called *uppers* or *downers*. We are being asked to "turn off and turn on," to get "high." These terms are, of course, part of the language of the streets. Well, which is it? Are we restoring equanimity to our troubled lives or are we "blowing our minds"? It depends, doesn't it?, on what you call it, and why.

This is why in discussing what words we shall use in describing an event, we are not engaging in "mere semantics." We are engaged in trying to control the perceptions and responses of others (as well as ourselves) to the character of the event itself. And that is why people who understand this fact wince when someone gets ready to "tell it like it is." No one can tell anything "like it is." In the first place, "it" isn't anything until someone names it. In the second place, the way in which "it" is named reveals not the way it *is* but how the namer wishes to see it or how he is capable of seeing it. And third, how it has been named becomes the reality for the namer and all who accept the name. But it need not be *our* reality.

Take, for example, the type of man who is conventionally called a *priest*. If you accept this name, you will not think him insane for deliberately abstaining from sexual intercourse for his entire lifetime. If you do not accept this name, you will think such a man is badly in need of psychiatric help. By "accepting" the name, I mean that you agree to its legitimacy, that you judge the semantic environment within which it occurs to be reasonable and purposeful. Above all, you accept the assumptions upon which it rests. Well, what shall we say, then, of "a priest"? How can we tell it like it really is? Is he displaying "psychotic symptoms" or is he displaying "his devotion to God"?

The point is well made in the story of the three umpires. The first umpire, being a man of small knowledge of how meanings are made, says, "I calls 'em as they are." The second umpire, knowing something about human perception and its limitations, says, "I calls 'em as I sees 'em." The third umpire, having studied at Cambridge with Wittgenstein himself, says, "Until I calls 'em, they ain't."

This does not mean, of course, that some umpires are not better than others. What you call something tells a great deal about how well and how widely you can see. After all, the umpire who calls "it" strike three, when everyone else sees the pitch sail over the batter's head, is usually called "blind." (It still counts as strike three, however.) J. Edgar Hoover may have named left turns (and Martin Luther King, as well) his nemesis, but the rest of us are not obliged to accept his labels.

And so, we have two matters to consider here. The first is a principle: The vocabulary of any semantic environment defines the reality with which the environment is concerned. The second is a question: How do we know when to accept or reject that vocabulary? As I am writing this chapter, a controversy is raging over whether or not the CIA has been implicated in political assassinations. The words "implicated in political assassinations" are not my words. They are the ones that the President and other "responsible officials" have used to talk about the subject (and, therefore, make it *into* the subject). So far as I know, no one (in public office) has asked if the CIA put out a "contract" on Fidel Castro, and, if it did, who the "hit" man was. This is the vocabulary of Albert (The Logical Positivist) Carillo, and, of course, makes "it" (i.e., attempts to terminate the lives of certain men) a different subject. *To assassinate* suggests entirely different motivations and a completely different context from *putting out a contract on*. In fact, the President of the United States (1975) has forthrightly stated that it is not the "policy" of his administration to assassinate. In other words, assassination is not a "crime"; it is a policy, which you may pursue or not, according to your needs.

There would be no "problem" here—no question of stupid or crazy talk—if not for people like George Orwell, who stand on the side and whisper troublesome words in our ears. For example: "Political language . . . is designed to make lies sound truthful and murder respectable." Or, as an example of how such language deceives (written about the Spanish Civil War, almost a quarter of a century *before* Vietnam): "Defenseless villages are bombarded from the air, the inhabitants driven out into the countryside, the cattle machine-gunned, the huts set on fire with incendiary bullets: this is called *pacification.* Millions of peasants are robbed of their farms and sent trudging along the roads with no more than they can carry: this is called *transfer of population* or *rectification of frontiers.*" Of course, I am not saying that Orwell, in accusing political leaders of murder, is "telling it like it is." He is telling it like he wants us to see it. And he wants us to see it that way because he regarded politics as a branch of moral philosophy. To Orwell, political language was doing what it is supposed to do when it revealed to people the moral implications of their actions. Even in cases where he participated in war (as in the Spanish Civil War) or gave his support to war (as in World War II), he refused to use words which would "depersonalize" the "enemy" or make war appear less than a brutal suspension of moral codes. Political language, he concluded, is largely a defense of the indefensible. But how shall we know if Orwell's way of seeing it is "right" or "wrong"? I wish there were an easy answer to this, but there isn't. There is, however, another principle—a rule, if you will—that is helpful.

I said a while back that what you call something depends on how well and widely you see. What I mean by this is that some people get "locked into" the vocabulary of a subject. By "locked in," I mean that they have so deeply internalized the words conventionally used to describe something that they seem unable even to imagine a different set of words being applied to the situation. Their perceptions are completely controlled by someone else's vocabulary. Such people are, then, at the mercy of someone else's names and at the mercy of the purposes that such names imply. Thus, the principle is that the more flexible you are in conceiving alternative names for things, the better will you be able to control your responses to situations. Make no mistake about it, the vocabulary of a semantic environment plays a critical role in setting the rules of response. If the President can get you to say, with him, that his administration's "policy" toward "assassinations" is such and such, then the such and such doesn't matter. You are in the same semantic environment as he, and the rest is mere commentary.

This principle does not imply that the vocabulary of every semantic environment is suspect. Some vocabularies are and some are not. The questions we need to ask are: What is the nature of the reality these words create? What sort of response do these words require of me? Does this response serve purposes with which I agree?

To Orwell, the language of politics ceased to serve any reasonable and humane purpose, and, as a consequence, he spent much of his time attacking its words and calling attention to the peculiar kinds of responses they required. But one does not need to go as far as Orwell to see that it is necessary to approach the vocabulary of certain systems with a full measure of skepticism. Such skepticism may profitably be displayed toward three aspects of the vocabulary of a semantic environment. The first I have already mentioned, and that is the technical, or specialized, words of a system.

A much more troublesome aspect of the vocabulary of a semantic environment is what I shall call its "key" words. By this, I mean those simple, nontechnical words which appear in every semantic environment but whose meanings shift as the words pass from one context to another. For example, it is not likely that you will have difficulty, if you are curious, in discovering the meanings of such terms as *Planck's constant* or *statute of limitations* or *extreme unction* or *ethnomethodological*. These are technical terms whose range of meaning is narrow and whose association with a particular universe of discourse is well fixed. But what of such words as true, false, right, wrong, law, progress, good, bad? Their potential for mischief is exceedingly great precisely because they do not appear to be technical terms, or "hard" words, and they are used in every system. The word *law*, for example, comes up in science, as in Newton's Law; in government, as in the law of the land, in religion, as in God's law; in economics, as in the law of supply and demand. And in the home, as in laying down the law. In each system, the meaning of "law" is quite special, and it is likely to confuse us unless we pay considerable attention to the assumptions on which the word rests.

Let us take a common example—the word *true*. What is a "true" statement in science? And how is it different from a "true" statement in politics? Or in literature? Or in law? Or in religion? And what of "progress"? Does a nation progress? And if it does, how is its progress different from progress in education, or sports, or science, or philosophy? Or, let us take one of the hardest words of all, *good*. "What is good for General Motors," Charles Wilson once said, "is good for America." Maybe so. But we would first have to know what *good* means in both parts of the sentence, and the meaning of each is buried deep in the soil of the semantic environment it comes from.

The first *good* comes from the world of business, and we can assume it refers to conditions which permit General Motors to increase its profits. But what does America "increase" by such conditions? Jobs, perhaps (but not necessarily). Air pollution, certainly. Better automobiles, perhaps (but not necessarily, and what would *better* mean?). More traffic jams, probably. In considering Mr. Wilson's proposition, we may wonder if there is any sense in which it can be said that something is "good" for "America." Whose America? And which Americans? And how do we determine in what sense something is "good" for it or them? In fact, one might even ask the same sort of question of General Motors. What is "good" for General Motors as viewed from the perspective of the United Auto Workers does not always coincide, as you may have noticed, with the meaning of *good* as understood by the chairman of the board.

But to come back to *America* for a moment: it is, naturally, a key word in many different semantic environments. "The Olympics is America's chance to show what it is made of," I heard a television announcer say recently. Ten minutes later, on another station, a preacher said, "There is a crisis of faith in America." Later that evening, an educator: "For all its faults, education in America is still the best." What aspect of "America" did each have in mind? Were they talking about particular Americans, or "America" in the abstract? And what sort of evidence, if any, did each use as the basis of the statement?

In each of these cases, I might add, it wouldn't surprise me if the audience was able to grasp the general sense in which the word was used, but how would any audience construe the term *un-American*? A House Committee on Treasonous Activities makes sense, even if unwarranted. A House Committee on Unpopular Opinions also makes sense, even if more unwarranted. But a House Committee on Un-American Activities? What could this mean? This term surely must be one of the more curious and revealing words in the semantic environment of politics. It suggests, to me at least, a religious aspect to citizenship, as if, in being an American citizen, one is committed to doctrines that are unknown or at least unaccepted outside our borders. I confess that if there are such doctrines, they have escaped my notice, so the term *un-American* remains a puzzle to me. But the main point here is not what puzzles or doesn't puzzle me, but how such seemingly simple, everyday words can generate such confusion.

A third aspect of the content of a semantic environment which requires our attention and Orwellian skepticism is what we may call its metaphors. Metaphor includes both technical terms and key words but may be distinguished by the fact that it imposes a precise kind of imagery or point of view on a subject or a situation. For example, when I talk about the process of communication, I tend to imagine it, as you know by now, as a biological process. And that is why I use such terms as *soil, environment, growth, pollution.* Those who imagine communication as a mechanical process will use such terms as *input, output, sender, receiver,* and *channel.* Each semantic environment is characterized by tendencies toward certain metaphorical constructions of reality. This is quite inevitable, but it also tends to be overlooked by those in the environment, and, on that account, can be quite dangerous. For example, when Walt Disney made his nature films, he quite explicitly anthropomorphized animals, that is, invested them with human qualities and motives. Most people have been quite aware of this, and I don't suppose that even the most devoted Disneyite is likely to expect that a deer or an otter, in spite of Disney's attributions, will enjoy playing cards or going skiing for a weekend. But, as Arthur Koestler has been trying to point out for years, most people are quite unaware of the opposite tendency in the work of many scientists, particularly behavioral psychologists. He calls this tendency *rattomorphic.* That is, a strong inclination to view the behavior of animals as the fundamental analog of the behavior of human beings. In the anthropomorphic view of nature, animals are held to act like men. In the rattomorphic view, men are held to act like animals. Rats are one of the more popular animals used but pigeons (B. F. Skinner), geese (Konrad Lorenz), and apes (Desmond Morris) have also been used as a basis for telling us what we are really like.

There is usually no "problem" here as long as one is aware that an analogy has been drawn. But frequently, workers in a certain field of activity or just plain people in ordinary situations allow their metaphors—through passion, forgetfulness, or ignorance—to get the better of them: Their perceptions get "locked into" a particular way of construing what is happening.

Among several reasons why the Women's Liberation Movement (an interesting metaphor in itself) runs into resistance is that both men and women have internalized a rich lexicon of metaphors about the subjects of sex, love, and domesticity. "A man's home is his castle," for example. Well, that makes him the king, doesn't it? And *she* is, of course, the queen. And kings beat queens, not only in kingdoms but in poker, as well. (And in chess, queens sacrifice themselves for kings, which is the proper thing to do.) Or how about a *working mother*, which rather suggests that the act of mothering is not work, while, for example, the act of waitressing is. Or how about not "tying your children to your apron strings"? Fathers are just as likely to do this as mothers, but since fathers are not apt to wear aprons, on whom does the onus fall? And how about *housewife* itself? This may not exactly imply that a woman marries a house, but it does suggest rather pointedly where she belongs. Or what about the *Miss* in *Miss Jones* (what exactly is Jones missing?). And who "wears the pants" in your family, anyway?

The "movement" is quite correct in challenging the

validity of these metaphors, especially because metaphors are apt to be so *unobtrusively* potent in giving direction to our attitudes. One might say that every political, scientific, social, religious, or economic "movement" represents an attack upon a prevailing set of metaphors, an established way of constructing reality. The divine right of kings was, after all, a metaphor which explained and justified a certain power relationship in government. Locke challenged the metaphor, Tom Paine ridiculed it, and Jefferson buried it, where it remained until Nixon almost restored it. In science, such a process of metaphor-challenge is commonplace. Classical physics, for example, relies heavily on the imagery of a billiard game. Its concepts of force, velocity, and position rest on the idea that atoms behave pretty much the way billiard balls do (the ballomorphic view of the universe?). Einstein, Bohr, and Heisenberg were the Locke, Paine, and Jefferson of the physical world. They "exposed" the limitations of the metaphor. The field of medicine, as Karl Menninger has been trying to teach us, relies to a considerable extent on the idea that disease is an alien force that "attacks" or "invades" human beings. While he concedes that some diseases are best described this way (for example, small-pox), there are many others which, apparently, require a different metaphor altogether. For instance, do we really "catch" a cold or do we "manufacture" it? Do we "contract" TB or "concoct" it? In the instance of ulcers, most of us are prepared to believe that we do not "catch" it; we "produce" it. But what of arthritis, cancer, rheu-matism? The search for cures will depend, to a large extent, on our finding new and illuminating metaphors. This is certainly the case in the field of psychiatry, where the prevailing metaphors have been under severe attack in recent years, most notably by Thomas Szasz and R. D. Laing. Is curious, bothersome, self-destructive behavior a "disease"? Is "mental illness" like "physical illness"? Or are "mentally disturbed" people "visionaries"?

I do not wish to imply that the metaphorical biases of every semantic environment are destructive, only that they are apt to be hard to see and therefore require close scrutiny. Scientists who refer to people as *subjects*, businessmen who refer to people as *personnel*, teachers who refer to people as *culturally disadvantaged* are not merely describing; they are committing themselves to a point of view, one of which they may be only dimly aware. (Years ago, I knew a man who owned a children's camp for which the season's fee was 500 dollars. The man referred to each of the campers as "my little half a G." In this instance, he knew quite well what his metaphor implied and rather reveled in it!)

It remains for me to say that no area of knowledge or social situation can exist without the support of metaphor. You will understand why if you look again at the sentence before this one. Why do I say knowledge is an "area"? Well, I could call it a "body," which suggests that it gets born, grows, and dies. Or I could call it a "realm," which suggests it has princes and peasants. But I will have to call it *something*, and that something must be drawn from my previous experience with the world around me. Simply, we think in metaphors. The question is, as Lewis Carroll stated it, who shall be the master?

Another principle governing the content of semantic environments is the *type* of sentence we expect from them. Each environment is characterized by certain types of sentences. In science, for example, we expect to find sentences that are mostly descriptive, predictive, and explanatory. In religion, we get sentences that are mostly prescriptive and judgmental—their function is to tell us what we ought to do and what we may think of ourselves if we do not do what we ought. In advertising, we find sentences that are also prescriptive and judgmental, although occasionally (and usually against the will of advertisers) a descriptive statement will be found; for example, "The surgeon general has determined that cigarette smoking is dangerous to your health." In a courtroom, a witness is required to confine himself to descriptive statements ("Please keep your conclusions to yourself, Mr. Harris, and just tell the court what you saw."); the judge is largely prescriptive ("I won't have any noise in this courtroom."); the jury is mostly evaluative ("We find the defendant, Mr. K., guilty."); and our greatest lawyers, e.g., Clarence Darrow, have always specialized in impressive explanatory sentences ("Mr. K. committed this crime, but we are all guilty for having been indifferent to the suffering that society has inflicted upon him."). I am, of course, oversimplifying the matter, since in most situations, including the courtroom, you will find a rich mixture of all kinds of sentences, representing the fullest range of reasons why people talk—to inform, to predict, to explain, to control, to find out, to judge, to persuade, and so on. These are not mutually exclusive. You can explain in order to control, or predict in order to persuade, or inform in order to judge. Even in a scientific environment, which is apt to be more rigorous than others in the kinds of sentences it will permit, you find instances of, for example, highly prescriptive statements.

Lysenko provides a notorious illustration of a scientist's believing that something *is* the case because he believed it *ought* to be the case. But the point is that while no semantic environment I can think of is confined to one or two types of sentences, there is usually an emphasis on certain types as against others. Astrology, as I have already explained, looks to me more like religion than science because the function of most of its sentences appears to be prescriptive rather than predictive. Religion, for its part, has had its craziest moments when it has tried to provide "scientific" descriptions of nature. It is exceedingly difficult to house both description and prescription in the same environment, as Copernicus, Galileo, and Kepler found out. One function is likely to pollute the other.

In some environments, of course, the question of what function of language shall predominate is highly controversial. In education, for example, arguments will frequently arise over whether teachers and textbooks should mainly prescribe and evaluate or mainly describe and explain. I used to have a firm opinion on this matter (favoring description and explanation), but I am no longer so sure.

In any case, there are two final points to be made about the types of sentences which comprise a semantic environment. The first is that when you have a situation where two seemingly different environments are dominated by virtually the same types of sentences, you had better look again to see if they are so different after all. For example, both religion and advertising almost wholly consist of prescriptive (this is what you *should* do) and evaluative (this is good and that is bad) statements. One may well wonder, then, if the purposes of these environments are more similar than different. Indeed, Billy Graham has packaged his "message" in a way not unlike that in which Scope packages its "message." In saying this, I am not sure if I am denigrating religion or elevating advertising. The point is this: The types of sentences we come across in each environment give us information about the purposes of the environment, and sometimes surprising information.

Second, it should be noted here that the function of sentences influences both their tone and their level of abstraction. Descriptive sentences, for example, tend to be cold and specific. Evaluative sentences, emotional and general. When we require a simple description, such as an answer to the question, "How do I get to Route 80 from here?" we do not expect an answer such as, "To get from here to there is like any journey of the soul, in which your character will be tested many times before you achieve tranquillity." Neither do we wish to hear a lecture on how and why means are more important than ends. There is a time for specificity and a time for abstractions, and a great deal of nonsense is generated by people who do not know what time it is. And speaking of that, it is time for me to say what I mean by both crazy talk and stupid talk.

Crazy Talk
Stupid Talk,

To the making of experts, there seems no end. To the unmaking, as well. When they disagree, as in Economics, there is confusion. When they agree, as in Vietnam, there is disaster. America, it sometimes appears, is dying from experts. But some of them have some breadth to their vision, and though their proposals are often grandiose, they are nonetheless interesting. Language experts, however, are apt to be obsessed with trivialities. For instance, I have before me some of the opinions of 136 such experts ("distinguished literary figures, commentators, and language experts," according to the editors of *The Harper Dictionary of Contemporary Usage*). They were asked to express their views on whether certain words and sentences were "right" or "wrong." In most cases, no context was provided for the words and sentences, so that the questions amounted to asking what their opinions are of the letters *t*, *f*, and *g*. It is as if someone had asked you what is your opinion of being handed a five-dollar bill. Even if you were an "expert" in international currency, you would be obliged to point out that this is a fairly empty question, and that everything would depend on the circumstances. If you had asked for change for a ten, one five-dollar bill would not be very satisfactory. But if you were broke, it might be breakfast, lunch, and dinner.

Apparently, the absence of a semantic context did not greatly trouble these experts, and off they went. "May *author* be a verb?" was one of the questions. Herman Wouk, who authored such classics as *Marjorie Morningstar*, said, "No, no, no, no, no, no, no! NO!" (What do you suppose he would have said to the question, "May one use eight *no*'s in a row?") Another question was whether or not the experts approved of *critique* as a transitive verb (as in, "The editor critiqued the college newspaper."). Michael J. Arlen said, "It sounds stupid." Since I greatly admire Arlen's work, I hoped that his *it* referred to the question itself, but, from the context, I was forced to conclude otherwise. To the same question, Mr. Wouk, who apparently used up all his best words in writing *Marjorie Morningstar*, said, "Yecch!" To the question, "May *alibi* be used for any kind of excuse?" Anthony Burgess replied, "*Alibi* means *somewhere else* to me. It can't mean one thing in Latin and law and another thing in nonlegal English." Mr. Burgess did not explain *why* a word "can't" mean one thing in one context and something else in another. He also, apparently, has not heard many Americans give alibis. Perhaps he has been somewhere else. But I would have gladly forgone his explanation of where he has been if he had explained the sense in which we are to construe his *can't.* Are we talking about violations of natural law? or social custom? or national pride? Or is this just Burgess' Law?

Most of the experts carried on in this trivial way, indicating their personal feelings about certain words *as words* ("I hate *five-dollar bills,*" "The letter *g* is an abomination," "*Ain't* is ugly," etc.). But a few of them gave replies of some social significance; for example, Leon Edel, a professor at New York University. To the question, "How about highway signs reading 'Go slow' (instead of 'slowly')?" Professor Edel replied, "*Slowly* would distract the illiterate."

Now, there are several things about this answer that are worth commenting on. In the first place, it is possibly illogical. If one takes *illiterate* to mean *unable to read,* then it wouldn't make much difference to an illiterate what the sign said. Second, his reply is possibly ignorant. If Edel means by *the illiterate* people who, let us say, prefer Jacqueline Susann to Henry James, and if he thinks that such people would be any more distracted by *ly* than he, then we can conclude he simply doesn't know what he's talking about. Which is very unusual for a professor from New York University. But third, and most important, Edel's remark, as illogical or ignorant (choose one) as it may be, is nonetheless one of the few opinions given by the experts which try to comment on the purpose and effect of this or any other sentence. He seems to have grasped the idea that the purpose of a road sign is to get people to *do* something, that it is important for them to do it, and that it is "bad" if they are distracted for some reason from doing it.

Thus, with Professor Edel's unwitting help, we can

locate the two central issues to consider in applying the names crazy talk and stupid talk. The first has to do with the purposes of a semantic environment and therefore concerns values. The second has to do with the effects or consequences of people's language, and therefore is a matter of "fact."

Crazy talk and stupid talk are names we may give to certain remarks whose usefulness we wish to call into question. And when we ask ourselves, what is it about such remarks that is worth challenging? the answer is something like this: Two major sources of trouble in human affairs are, first, that people use language for "bad" (inhumane, unattainable) purposes, and second, people use language ineffectively in trying to achieve "good" purposes. We are not talking in this book about words and sentences. We are talking about what they are *for* and how well they *do* what they are for.

So far, wherever I have used the term *crazy talk*, I have been referring to talk that reflects "bad" purposes. Where I have used the term *stupid talk*, I have been referring to talk that defeats legitimate purposes. Now, I will not say that this taxonomy is especially rigorous. It certainly has the potential for confusion, especially since it is so difficult to say what are the purposes of a situation, let alone whether they are "good" or "bad." But after all, when you consider that a whale is not classified as a fish (which it certainly *looks* like) and a tomato is not classified as a vegetable (which it certainly is *used* as), you must concede that any attempt to classify anything poses difficulties. In this case, my distinction between crazy talk and stupid talk is no less precise or more troublesome than a psychiatrist's distinction between a "manic-depressive" and a "schizophrenic." And I bother to make the distinction for the same reason: It helps in pointing the way to a solution to the "problem." If we can see, even dimly, the way in which some person or situation is not working, then we are better equipped to suggest remedies. Here, I want to remind you again that in using the terms *crazy talk* and *stupid talk*, I am not saying that people *are* crazy or *are* stupid. I am talking about language which, in particular situations, does not or cannot achieve reasonable and humane purposes, either because the purpose is unreasonable and inhumane or the language will not do what it is supposed to do.

Let us take as a first example, then, the matter which Professor Edel has called to our attention. I place it here because, frankly, it is simple and will give a clear picture of the difference between crazy and stupid talk. To begin with, I think I may say without fear of contradiction that the purpose of road signs is to inform drivers of highway regulations and, therefore, to decrease the chances of accident. I will go further and say that this is a perfectly legitimate purpose. I cannot prove that it is, since statements of value cannot be proven. But I *can* say that efforts to increase the prospects of human survival almost always seem desirable to me, and not only to me but to many people throughout the world. I am aware, of course, that not *all* people agree with this proposition, even in relation to the highways. I have seen, for example, the work of "vandals" who have painted a "3" into an "8," so that a road sign will say, "Speed limit 85 miles." This is what I call crazy talk, since its conscious purpose is to increase rather than diminish accidents. Stupid talk is a rather different matter. Let us assume that the state highway department—for example, in Connecticut—is committed to human survival. We can then assume that its road signs will be exclusively devoted to that end and that the words which comprise them will be clear to the great majority of drivers. Professor Edel is surely wrong in believing that "illiterates" (Jacqueline Susann variety) would be distracted by "go slowly," but I do know several drivers who *have* been distracted by "No crossing the median divider," which is a favorite of someone in the Connecticut State Highway Department. The phrase *median divider* is a good example of stupid talk, since it has the potential to confuse at least some drivers (maybe even readers of Henry James) and therefore defeats the basic purpose of a sign.

As you know, the language of road signs is almost entirely dominated by prescriptive sentences, such as "Go slow," "No left turn," "Stop here," "Hitchhiking prohibited." I have sometimes thought that this type of sentence might be the cause of some resentment on the part of drivers who, whether on the road of life or the road to Danbury, do not fancy being given orders. It has crossed my mind that compliance might be more easily effected if highway regulations were stated in the form of predictive statements, such as, "If you exceed 50 miles per hour and are observed doing this by a state trooper, the chances are great that you will be given a speeding ticket." I think Professor Edel would like that statement. And so would I, since its tone is more suitable to the kind of relationship government ought to have with citizens. But at 50 miles per hour, it would certainly be hard to read, and at 70, just about impossible.

In any case, the semantic environment of road signs

rarely, if ever, produces crazy talk, since just about everyone grants the legitimacy of its purpose. If we are to have problems in this environment, they will come from stupid talk, such as the suggestion I made in the last paragraph.

Our next example, however, presents a somewhat different situation. The language in question is as follows: "Nothing terrible is going to happen to you. All you have to do is to breathe in deeply. That strengthens the lungs. Inhaling is a means of preventing infectious diseases." Sounds like Marcus Welby giving assurances to a TB patient, doesn't it? The next sentences will tell you that it isn't: "The men will have to work building houses and roads. But the women won't be obliged to do so; they'll do housework or help in the kitchen." (The question for the experts is, "Can *but* be used as the first word of a sentence?") This little specimen of human language is the greeting given by an SS man to a trainload of Jews who had arrived at the gas-chamber complex at Belzec in August 1942. There is nothing stupid about this language since it was generally effective in reducing the possibility of a desperate rebellion by the new arrivals. It is, however, crazy talk because of the context in which it occurred. It was part of a pervasive semantic environment whose strategy was to make genocide appear reasonable.

A similar example of this is found in a remark made by Paul Blobel, who was responsible for the massacre of 30,000 Jews and Russians at Babi Yar, near Kiev. Blobel, incidentally, was a university graduate of delicate sensibilities. Grammarians and other guardians of the purity of language will be pleased to know he had, in his small way, a commitment to their cause. Nonetheless, in explaining at Nuremberg what happened at Babi Yar, he said, "Human life was not as valuable to them [i.e., the Russians and Jews] as to us. Our men who took part in these executions suffered more than those who had to be shot." It is fairly certain that Blobel believed this, as did many others. But to get men to speak such sentences, you must first create a context in which language itself has got loose from its moorings, a context in which language no longer connects with rational purposes. The question of the effectiveness of such language is irrelevant. One might even say that the sentence asserting that those *behind* the rifles are suffering more than those *in front* is a brilliant one—if your purpose is to persuade yourself and others that you are not wantonly insane.

Talk is stupid when it does not work. Talk is crazy when, in working, it creates and sustains an irrational purpose.

These two examples were chosen largely because they so easily demonstrate the distinction I am trying to make. But here is one that is somewhat more complicated. You will remember that Gordon Cooper was an astronaut, shot up above buildings and into outer space. During his seventeenth orbit around the Earth, he was moved to say a prayer. It is as follows:

> I would like to take this time to say a little prayer for all people, including myself, involved in this launch operation. Father, thank You, especially for letting me fly this flight. Thank You for the privilege of being able to be in this position; to be up in this wondrous place, seeing all these many startling, wonderful things that You have created.

Help guide and direct all of us, that we may shape
our lives to be much better Christians, trying to help
one another, and to work with one another rather than
fighting and bickering. Help us to complete this mission
successfully. Help us in our future space endeavors, that
we may show the world that a democracy really can
compete, and still are able to do things in a big way, and
are able to do research, development, and can conduct
many scientific and very technical programs.

Be with all our families. Give them guidance and encouragement, and let them know that everything will be
O.K.

We ask in Thy name. Amen.

I will, of course, ignore Cooper's grammatical errors
and other trivial improprieties, since they have no bearing on what is important here (and because even Herman Wouk might get a little dizzy and slip a bit on *his*
seventeenth orbit around the Earth). What *is* important
in judging the character of Cooper's language is the function of prayer, and how Cooper performs it. People pray,
of course, for many reasons, but I think it fair to say that
the principal motive is to give form and substance to the
belief that there is a transcendent purpose to life, embodied in a concept or deity which has dominion over
all things. Through prayer, people put their ambitions,
successes, failures, and tragedies in perspective. They
humble themselves before greater powers and, by so
doing, frequently find themselves uplifted and stronger.
Again, I cannot prove it, but this seems to me a worthwhile purpose, and is, at least, widely practiced by civilized people all over the world. Cooper, then, is not
doing anything that could be judged to be unreasonable

or harmful. This does not appear to be crazy talk. More-over, there is, at least for me, a certain charm, if not poignancy, in the fact that Cooper elected at that mo-ment to say a prayer, as if he meant to imply that though the Tower of Babel be built, men still know they are only men and not gods. And yet it seems to me that this is one of the stupidest prayers I have ever heard. It is so stupid, in fact, that its purpose is more than defeated or compromised. It is completely transformed. And, as a consequence, we may have here a case of stupid and crazy talk at the same time.

To begin with, if you look again at his prayer, you will see a curious contradiction between its tone and its con-tent. Its attitude and role-structure are clearly recogniz-able as those of prayer. With the exception of the first sentence, in which he announces what he is going to do and whom he is going to do it for, every sentence begins, basically, with either a "thank you" or a request for help. He is, in other words, a supplicant, which is the role and tone always employed in prayer. But when you try to identify the object of Cooper's supplication (that is, *who* would be interested in helping with the problems he mentions), the alternatives that come to mind are curious. The first is the secretary of defense, who would certainly be more interested than any god I have ever heard of in how America makes out in its space en-deavors. Another might be professors of political theory, who might be interested in whether or not "a democracy" can compete (for example, with totalitarian states) and do things in a big way. A third might be the American taxpayer, through whose money NASA is able to con-duct many technical and scientific programs. (If it *is* the taxpayer, then Cooper obviously means to appeal only to those taxpayers who are Christians.) I hope you understand that I have no objection to Cooper's anthropomorphizing God, to his imagining a humanlike deity who rules the universe. It is not the fact *that* he has imagined; it is *what* he has imagined. What it comes down to, in Cooper's prayer, is that God is an American, taxpaying Christian who supports the space program, favors democratic political systems, wants more research done, and, for all we know, believes in publish or perish. In Cooper's construct of God, not only does God *not* rule over the universe and all that's in it. He doesn't even rule over Yugoslavia. In short, though it takes the form of a prayer, Cooper's language is a celebration of America's supremacy, not God's. It is dominated by the language of politics, not religion. In substance, it lacks many things that a prayer should contain, including transcendence, universality, and especially an acknowledgment of God's majestic indifference to the political maneuvers of a particular group of people. Is it crazy talk or stupid talk? I would be inclined to the former. But you must keep in mind that these terms do not refer to "real" things, in the sense that eyeglasses or cigarettes are "real." They are intended, in fact, to suggest a *direction* toward which we might look in order to find what is "wrong," either with a person's use of language or with the situation in which it is used.

If, in constructing such a prayer, Cooper was merely reflecting his own limitations, we would have a fairly clear example of stupid talk. He would simply be telling us that he does not really know what a prayer consists of, beyond that it requires one to say "Father," "amen," and a few other technical words. But there is some evidence that this impoverished conception of religion is widely shared by other people. There were certainly many citizens who were deeply moved by Cooper's prayer. This suggests that we live in a land where the goals of the state are increasingly identified with the goals of God. And for that reason, I say that Cooper's prayer is not so much a matter of ineffectiveness but of a general tendency in the culture to obliterate the distinction between the language of politics and the language of religion (a tendency promoted, incidentally, by both "right-wing" clerics, e.g., the late Francis Cardinal Spellman, and "left-wing" clerics, e.g., William Sloane Coffin). Here, you will notice, I am introducing another parameter to the difference between stupid and crazy talk. Stupid talk is apt to be an expression of individual weakness—a failure on the part of one person to see what a semantic environment is supposed to do, and how it does it. Stupid talk usually has no implications beyond the immediate situation, and is often correctable by someone's calling attention to unanticipated consequences. In thinking that cars make left turns, and that they make them badly, J. Edgar Hoover was talking stupid, not crazy. The sentence "There shall be no left turns made by this car" is not one that resonates throughout the culture. But the sentence "God is an American, and, in any case, is not a Communist" *is* such a sentence. In my way of thinking, it is crazy talk. It has implications for several semantic environments, tending to extinguish the differences among them. It is a sentence that impoverishes a culture, not merely an individual. You might even say that stupid talk is a question of individual error, while crazy talk is a question of collective error. As in the following example:

> Sometimes people get the notion that the purpose of est is to make you better. It is not. I happen to think that you are perfect exactly the way you are. . . . The problem is that people get stuck acting the way they were instead of being the way they are.

Or, you might say, vice versa.

This specimen is an example of the language of therapy (Instant Variety) and comes out of the mouth of Werner Erhard, who is the founder of Erhard Seminars Training (est). Erhard has also said:

> The purpose of est training is to transform your ability to experience living so that the situations you have been trying to change or have been putting up with clear up just in the process of living.

Thousands of people have enrolled in est, and not a few have claimed that they no longer act the way they were and, instead, spend their time being the way they are. They pay a fair amount of money to learn what that *just* is in the last quote, and they learn it in 60 hours of more or less continuous "training." According to Mel Ziegler, of the *San Francisco Chronicle*, this training consists largely of

> interminable, scatologically cluttered harangues, driving again and again at what clearly emerged as The Point:

That the "trainees" in the room were all 'a------' [*sic*] because they had brought on themselves everything that
had ever gone wrong for them in their lives.

Now I do not say that some of these "esters" do not,
in fact, feel better when they have finished giving their
money and attention to est's trainers. I do not know the
percentage of "success," although it should be pointed
out that about 50 percent of all patients who enter
"mental" hospitals improve, i.e., feel better, no matter
what sort of "treatment" they get, and even if they get
none. There is no telling what will make some people
"feel" better. Sometimes a lobster dinner will do it, or a
raise in pay, or even reading a good book. Of course,
meeting a lot of fellows and girls also helps. The point
I wish to stress here is that the "helpfulness" of Erhard's
language is largely beside the point. If you tell people
that they are "perfect" except for the way they act, that
"just" the process of living will clear up their problems,
that they have brought on "everything" that has ever
gone wrong for them, and that what they "are" is not
reflected in what they do, you may (for all I know)
make quite a lot of distracted people feel good. You will
also have shown, once again, that Edmund Burke was
wrong. When all else fails, people do not turn to reason.
They usually turn to gibberish.

I have no doubt that many individuals have received
"spiritual sustenance" from ESP stories, numerology, the
burning of witches, astrology, exorcism, mumbling to
themselves, messages from outer space, and other higher
forms of consciousness. I am equally sure that Hitler
made many discontented Germans feel good about them-

selves. The Inquisition probably did wonders for Christians, and bombing the Vietnamese back to the Stone Age was quite possibly a "peak experience" for millions of Americans. And while I do not mean to compare est to any of the hideous events I have just mentioned, it must take its humble place in the spacious museum of crazy talk. For though crazy talk comes in many varieties and magnitudes, it is, essentially, an attack on reason itself. It may cloak its purposes as science or religion or therapy or politics, but its most profound strategy is to by-pass or defy our capacity to reason. And that capacity, as Spinoza taught, is the source of all ethical behavior. It is also the one talent lodged in us whose denial makes us less human.

The problem of crazy talk, in other words, is not in what it does *for* you but in what it does *to* you. Crazy talk, even in its milder forms, requires that we be mystified, suspend critical judgment, accept premises without question, and (frequently) abandon entirely the idea that language ought to be connected with reality.

According to the *San Francisco Chronicle*, Erhard typically speaks in the following manner (talking to one of his trainers):

> Ted, I haven't yet had the space to tell you this, but I want to acknowledge that I'm clear about your appropriate contribution in helping resolve Stewart's immigration problems. And Don (Cox, who runs the business of est) will validate the mechanical part of helping you experience my acknowledgment.

Ziegler interprets this to mean: "Ted, you did a nice job with Stewart's immigration, and I told Don to give you a bonus." He may be right, but I'm not sure. Erhard, for his part, says that such talk is

> incredibly useful and actually important when you are describing something that's new, because what it does is it allows people to know that you're not describing something that is old.

Or vice versa.

Now, it is clear that Erhard's way of talking is far from stupid. He has made quite a lot of money from sentences such as these, and that is the point: He has struck a rich vein in the culture—the tendency to separate words from any specific referents, to make gibberish itself into a semantic environment. Such a tendency can be seen in advertising, government, radical politics, astrology, guruism, instant therapies, and other forms of popular entertainment. When one person uses rootless language, we might think of it as stupid talk. But when a fairly large population responds enthusiastically to it, when we find a whole subculture adopting the same pattern, it is useful to think of it as crazy talk. For what we are faced with is not an aberrant remark but an aberrant semantic environment.

The "problem" of crazy talk is, therefore, very close to uncorrectable. It does not involve a momentary loss of judgment, subject to review in a more rational moment. Crazy talk usually puts forward a point of view that is considered virtuous and progressive. Its assumptions, metaphors, and conclusions are therefore taken for granted, and that, in the end, is what makes it crazy.

For it is language that cannot get outside of itself. It buries itself in its own foundations.

Here, for example, is a specimen taken from *Red Stocking's Manifesto*:

> Women are an oppressed class. Our oppression is total, affecting every facet of our lives. We are exploited as sex objects, breeders, domestic servants, and cheap labor.... We identify the agents of our oppression as men. Male supremacy is the oldest, most basic form of domination. All other forms of exploitation (racism, capitalism, imperialism, etc.) are extensions of male supremacy....

Before saying anything about this language, I think I ought to make it plain that I believe in the equality of the sexes, that no female should be denied whatever opportunities are available to males. I mention this because it is in the nature of most "isms" (and "ologies") that criticism of any part of the "ism" reflects a rejection of the whole. Therefore, one is required to show one's colors, so to speak, before one may offer criticism of any sort.

Having said that, I feel somewhat more comfortable in remarking that the language I have just quoted is in some respects not far removed from Paul Blobel's analysis of the events at Babi Yar. If you talk about Russians and Jews as subhuman beings, you have created a context in which you are incapable of knowing what they experience. And if you talk about men as "total oppressors" and women as "totally exploited," you have constructed a context that bears almost no relation to the actual experience of men and women. Crazy talk is, in fact, almost always characterized by simple-minded conceptions of complex relationships.

One way it achieves this is through the construction of a massive metaphor which permeates every sentence and does not allow for any perceptions that go beyond the bounds of the metaphor. In the foregoing instance, we are presented with a vicious and uncompromising paradigm: Man–woman relationships are a war between master and slave. It follows from this that a woman who gives birth to a child is a "breeder." And a woman who stays home with children while her husband works is a "domestic servant" and "cheap labor." It follows, as well, that there can be no such thing as "mutual dependency" or "love" or even a "family," since such transactions do not arise in a class war. It also follows that it is only an illusion that some men have sacrificed their own well-being for their families, since masters do not do such things for slaves.

In short, to talk this way is to distort, beyond recognition, a complex situation as it is actually experienced by most men and women.

Of course, the passage I am discussing represents an extreme position. But what makes a position "extreme"? It is language that settles a matter once and for all, language that does not take into account contradiction and ambiguity, language which eagerly suppresses facts that do not fit its premises, language that is self-confirming. The self-confirming aspect of crazy talk is particularly interesting. For example, it is sometimes asserted that a man's referring to his wife as "my wife" or "my woman" demonstrates the truth of the claim that marriage is a simple master–slave relationship. But the word *my* is an extremely complicated word and in fact may demonstrate exactly the opposite of what is claimed for it. When you say of what is on your wrist that it is "my watch," you certainly mean that you own it. It is yours to do with as you wish. But when you say of where you live that it is "my country," you mean almost the opposite. For, if anything, it is the country that owns you. Certainly, in talking of *our God*, we do not imply that we own Him, but just the opposite.

Whatever the phrase *my wife* may have implied a hundred years ago, not even Archie Bunker would take it to mean a simple case of ownership today. For most people, I would imagine it is a statement of commitment to or responsibilities for another person.

In any case, the relationships between men and women are characterized not only by antagonisms and inequalities but by acts of great sacrifice, tenderness, and devotion. And I would say that any language pattern which excludes the sacrifice, tenderness, and devotion in the framework of marriage is a form of crazy talk, a lowering, not a raising, of consciousness. It is one thing to say that there are still imbalances and inequities in this relationship. It is quite another to say that in marriage, men own their women, to do with as they will, for the general purpose of keeping them oppressed. The first can lead to inquiry and action. The second is a propagandistic distortion of great destructive power.

Stupid talk is an individual mistake whose unfortunate consequences are usually immediate and observable by others within the semantic environment. This does not mean that there can be no argument about it. *Stupid talk* is still an opinion given by one fallible human being about the remarks of another fallible human being. But because the semantic environment itself is not in question, stupid talk is limited in its scope, and its presence may be detected in the fact that something that ought to have happened hasn't, or something that ought not to have happened has. Rarely does it involve fundamental questions of value, and for that reason, stupid talk is often easy to correct, or, at least, to avoid next time.

Crazy talk, on the other hand, grows from a challenge to the semantic environment itself. It establishes different purposes and assumptions from those we normally accept. It has, therefore, wide-ranging consequences and is a form of collectivized nonsense. Crazy talk cannot, of course, be verified or refuted by facts. You cannot prove that putting people in gas chambers even lacks charm, let alone humanity. And you cannot prove that love or marriage ought to be something more than a class war, or that appeals to God ought somehow to be different from the Pledge of Allegiance. You can only assert these things and try to show how their denial is destructive to the human enterprise. I have previously stated, for example, that a society's "health" depends on its having clearly differentiated purposes. There is no way to "prove" that this is so, except in a long-range view, and even then, there are philosophers who will argue the opposite. But as you have concluded by now, my definitions of both stupid and crazy talk stand or fall on certain commonplace normative concepts. For example, I hypothesize a world in which road signs are made clear because it is desirable to reduce accidents; a world in which gas chambers are thinkable only by people gone mad; a world in which prayer expresses obeisance to God, not the State; a world in which no one is "perfect" and in which there are no sixty-hour therapies to remedy the troubles of life, least of all therapies involving the blaming of oneself for "everything." And I hypothesize a world in which men and women come together to overcome the alienation that separateness brings and not to overcome each other.

You will agree, I think, that there is nothing novel in such values, although you may think them ill-conceived. Wherever you do think them unwarranted, at that point will my conception of stupid and crazy talk be both unacceptable and useless to you. But there must be a standard of human behavior against which we can measure what we say and do. I like thinking that mine, in general, reflects the idea contained in Jacob Bronowski's line that "we are nature's unique experiment to make the rational intelligence prove itself sounder than the reflex." In the five chapters you have now completed, I have been trying to suggest what that line means to me. But I am not yet finished doing it. In Part 2, I will catalogue some of the specific mechanisms and myths through which the "rational intelligence" is defeated and our reflexes helped to gain dominion. When you have read Part 2, you will understand my values more clearly and be able to decide how to construe the advice I give in Part 3. Or whether or not to bother with it at all.

PART

2

Introduction

"Therefore it seemeth to me, that the truest way to understand conversation, is to know the faults and errors to which it is subject, and from thence every man to form maxims to himself whereby it may be regulated. . . ."

JONATHAN SWIFT
Hints Toward an Essay on Conversation

The faults and errors to which Swift is here referring include talking too much, talking too much about yourself, and pedantry, which he defines as attaching too much importance to your knowledge (whether that knowledge be philosophy or cooking). These are certainly elementary talking errors and may properly be called stupid talk since, as Swift predicts, they invariably have the effect of achieving almost the exact opposite of what the speaker intends.

In the section that follows, there is no discussion of

these particular errors, nor is there any discussion of several others that might easily come to mind. I have included only those "faults and errors" which impress me as the most serious obstacles to the achievement of effective discourse within a rational semantic environment.

If, up to this point, my discussion of stupid and crazy talk has been too general or even ambiguous, then I offer the following seventeen small chapters as a remedy. They form my operational definition of stupid and crazy talk. They analyze certain beliefs, habits of speech, and structural characteristics of language which play an indispensable role in the production of nonsense of all sizes and shapes.

The Communication
Panacea

In the search for the Holy Grail of complete harmony, liberation, and integrity, which it is the duty of all true Americans to conduct, adventurers have stumbled upon a road sign which appears promising. It says, in bold letters, **"All problems arise through lack of communication."** Under it, in smaller print, it says: "Say what is on your mind. Express your feelings honestly. This way lies the answer." A dangerous road, it seems to me. It is just as true to say, This way lies disaster.

I would not go so far as Oliver Goldsmith, who observed that the principal function of language is to *conceal* our thoughts. But I do think that concealment is one of the important functions of language, and on no account should it be dismissed categorically. As I have tried to make clear earlier, semantic environments have legitimate and necessary purposes of their own which do not always coincide with the particular and pressing needs of every individual within them. One of the main purposes of many of our semantic environments, for example, is to help us maintain a minimum level of civility in conducting our affairs. Civility requires not that we deny our feelings, only that we keep them to ourselves when they are not relevant to the situation at hand. Contrary to what many people believe, Freud does not teach us that we are "better off" when we express our deepest feelings. He teaches exactly the opposite: that civilization is impossible without inhibition. Silence, reticence, restraint, and, yes, even dishonesty can be great virtues, in certain circumstances. They are, for example, frequently necessary in order for people to work together harmoniously. To learn how to say no is important in achieving personal goals, but to learn how to say yes when you want to say no is at the core of civilized behavior. There is no dishonesty in a baboon cage, and yet, for all that, it holds only baboons.

Now there are, to be sure, many situations in which trouble develops because some people are unaware of what other people are thinking and feeling. "If I'd only *known* that!" the refrain goes, when it is too late. But there are just as many situations which would get worse, not better, if everyone knew exactly what everyone else was thinking. I have in mind, for example, a conflict over school busing that occurred some time ago in New York City but has been replicated many times in different places. Whites against blacks. The whites maintained that they did not want their children to go to other neighborhoods. They wanted them close at hand, so that the children could walk home for lunch and enjoy all the benefits of a "neighborhood school." The blacks maintained that the schools their children attended were

THE COMMUNICATION PANACEA 99

run-down and had inadequate facilities. They wanted their children to have the benefits of a good educational plant. It was most fortunate, I think, that these two groups were not reduced to "sharing with each other" their real feelings about the matter. For the whites' part, much of it amounted to, "I don't want to live, eat, or do anything else with niggers. Period." For the blacks' part, some of it, at least, included, "You honky bastards have had your own way at my expense for so long that I couldn't care less what happens to you or your children." Had these people communicated such feelings to each other, it is more than likely that there could have been no resolution to this problem. (This seems to have been the case in Boston.) As it was, the issue could be dealt with *as if* such hatred did not exist, and therefore, a reasonable political compromise was reached.

It is true enough, incidentally, that in this dispute and others like it, the charge of racism was made. But the word *racism*, for all its ominous overtones, is a euphemism. It conceals more than it reveals. What Americans call a *racist* public remark is something like "The Jews own the banks" or "The blacks are lazy." Such remarks are bad enough. But they are honorifics when compared to the "true" feelings that underlie them.

I must stress that the "school problem" did not arise in the first place through lack of communication. It arose because of certain historical, sociological, economic, and political facts which could not be made to disappear through the "miracle of communication." Sometimes, the less people know about other people, the better off everyone is. In fact, political language at its best can be viewed as an attempt to find solutions to problems by circumventing the authentic hostile feelings of concerned parties.

In our personal lives, surely each of us must have ample evidence by now that the capacity of words to exacerbate, wound, and destroy is at least as great as their capacity to clarify, heal, and organize. There is no good reason, for example, for parents always to be honest with their children (or their children always to be honest with them). The goal of parenthood is not to be honest, but to raise children to be loving, generous, confident, and competent human beings. Where full and open revelation helps to further that end, it is "good." Where it would defeat it, it is stupid talk. Similarly, there is no good reason why your boss always needs to know what you are thinking. It might, in the first place, scare him out of his wits and you out of a job. Then, too, many of the problems you and he have do not arise from lack of communication, but from the nature of the employer–employee relationship, which sometimes means that the less money you make, the more he does. This is a "problem" for a labor organizer, not a communication specialist.

Some large American corporations have, of late, taken the line that "improved communication" between employees and management will solve important problems. But very often this amounts to a kind of pacification program, designed to direct attention away from fundamental economic relationships. It is also worth noting that a number of such corporations have ceased to hold "communication seminars" in which executives were encouraged to express their "true" feelings. What happened, apparently, is that some of them decided they hated their jobs (or each other) and quit. Whether this is "good" or not depends on your point of view. The corporations don't think it's so good, and probably the families of the men don't either.

The main point I want to make is that "authentic communication" is a two-edged sword. In some circumstances, it helps. In others, it defeats. This is a simple enough idea, and sensible people have always understood it. I am stressing it here only because there has grown up in America something amounting to a holy crusade in the cause of Communication. One of the terms blazoned on its banners is the phrase *real* (or *authentic*) feelings. Another is the motto "Get in touch with your feelings!" From what I have been able to observe, this mostly means expressing anger and hostility. When is the last time someone said to you, "Let me be *lovingly* frank"? The expression of warmth and gentleness is usually considered to be a facade, masking what you are really thinking. To be certified as authentically in touch with your feelings, you more or less have to be nasty. Like all crusades, the Communication Crusade has the magical power to endow the most barbarous behavior with a purity of motive that excuses and obscures just about all its consequences. No human relationship is so tender, apparently, that it cannot be "purified" by sacrificing one or another of its participants on the altar of "Truth." Or, to paraphrase a widely known remark on another subject, "Brutality in the cause of honesty needs no defense." The point is that getting in touch with your feelings often amounts to losing touch with the feelings of others. Or at least losing touch with the purposes for which people have come together.

A final word on the matter of "honesty." As I have said

before, human purposes are exceedingly complex—multi-leveled and multilayered. This means that, in any given situation, one does not have *an* "honest feeling," but a whole complex of different feelings. And, more often than not, some of these feelings are in conflict. If anger predominates at one instant, this does not mean it is more "authentic" than the love or sorrow or concern with which it is mingled. And the expression of the anger, alone, is no less "dishonest" than any other partial representation of what one is feeling. By *dishonesty*, then, I do not merely mean saying the opposite of what you believe to be true. Sometimes it is necessary to do even this in the interests of what you construe to be a worthwhile purpose. But more often, dishonesty takes the form of your simply not saying *all* that you are thinking about or feeling in a given situation. And, since our motives and feelings are never all that clear, to our own eyes in any case, most of us are "dishonest" in this sense most of the time. To be aware of this fact and to temper one's talk in the light of it is a sign of what we might call "intelligence." Other words for it are discretion and tact.

The relevant point is that communication is most sensibly viewed as a means through which desirable ends may be achieved. As an end in itself, it is disappointing, even meaningless. And it certainly does not make a very good deity.

Fanaticism

The commonplace image of fanaticism is of an arm-waving hysteric preaching a mad and unholy doctrine. If this were all there were to it, we could dismiss it in a paragraph. Not because it isn't dangerous, but because it is so obvious. But fanaticism has many forms, of which wild-eyed hysteria is only the most audible. Some of its deadliest faces have a much quieter aspect. The picture that most readily comes to my mind is that of an experiment conducted many times with minnows and pike. Both species are put in a large tank but are kept separate from each other by a glass shield. The pike, being very fond of eating minnows, go for them immediately but, of course, bump into the glass partition. The pike keep trying—five times, ten times, in some cases, many more. Then, they give up. At that point, the glass partition is removed so that the minnows swim freely amidst the pike who are hungrier than ever. What happens next? The pike will not eat the minnows. Pike will even starve to death under such conditions.

If we were to anthropomorphize the pike, we might say that they are guilty of crazy talk. They have become fixated on a single sentence, "The minnows are not available." The sentence originated in a context in which it was both demonstrably true and useful. With the context completely changed, the sentence lingers on, though it is now both demonstrably false and dangerous. Our pike, it seems, are a bunch of depressed, suicidal fanatics.

To the minnows, of course, this fanaticism is a god-send, and, if Disney were portraying the scene, I could imagine his putting a small, maybe demonic, smile on the faces of the minnows. One fish's fanaticism is an-other's salvation. But in human affairs, fanaticism rarely has a redeeming side. It affects everyone in a semantic environment and makes the pursuit of intelligent purpose extremely difficult.

Fanaticism begins with our falling in love, so to speak, with certain sentences. There is nothing unusual in this. Neither is there anything especially dangerous, provided we are willing to permit the sentences to be scrutinized, subjected to criticism, and revised as their deficiencies require. But as with most love affairs, the object of our affection is a projection of our own needs, and we will not hear criticism of any sort—at least for a while. That we have nothing in common with our lover, or that he or she will make us into something it is not in our best interests to become is the sort of observation one can make only if detachment and examination are not viewed as threats. Fanaticism is the internalization of sentences to which we are so attached that we have made them immune to criticism. Not only by others, but by ourselves, as well. Ironically, our very attachment to such sentences disgraces them, as your lover would be disgraced if you did not permit him or her to be scrutinized by others.

The archetypical fanatical response is given in the story about the man who believed he was dead. In an effort to release him from this idea, a psychiatrist asked him if dead men bleed. "Of course not," he replied, whereupon the psychiatrist jabbed the man's finger with a pin so that they both could see the rich, red blood flow. The man looked at the blood, at the psychiatrist, and then said, "Well, I'll be damned, dead men *do* bleed!"

Now, there is an important difference between our bleeding dead man and our starving pike. The pike began with a sentence that was true. The man began with one that is false. Like the pike, men certainly plague themselves with once-true sentences that have become false through changing conditions. But men can also invent sentences that have no truth in them and never have, which is generally not the case with animals, whose "beliefs" are closely connected with the specific requirements of their survival. The ability to conceive of false ideas is man's most important power; it is that which distinguishes us most from the animal world and which grants us such wide dominion. To think of an idea that only might be true or that nature manifestly contradicts is quite beyond the capacity of a mako shark. In the environment of the sea, a lure and a fishhook are a false idea, which because the shark has limited imagination, appear to it quite as useful as anything else. To conjecture and speculate and hypothesize about what might be so, even if it is not, is eventually the source of all good ideas. But such power is an affliction if not balanced by the power to refute and discard. Fanaticism is what happens when the will to refute deserts you.

This idea—that human intelligence is engaged in its most functional activity when in the process of refutation—has been given sophisticated expression by the philosopher Karl Popper. He calls his point of view "fallibilism." It proceeds from the simple assumptions that all people and their ideas are fallible, and that it is not possible for anyone to know if he or she is in possession of the "truth." Therefore, to devote oneself to justifying one's beliefs is, essentially, an act of fanaticism and the source of much cruelty and injustice. Popper proposes instead an attitude of "critical rationalism," which requires that we subject our beliefs to constant criticism in the hope of reducing the extent of their error. In another place, Charles Weingartner and I have called this attitude "crap detecting," which tells you that we come from a different neighborhood from Popper's. Other than that, "critical rationalism" and "crap detecting" amount to the same thing. They are opposed to the "justificationist" position, which leads people to seek reasons why they *should* believe something. The idea is to seek reasons why one *should not* believe something. In Popper's view, the history of science is the history of detecting false beliefs, not the history of discovering true beliefs. The significant demarcation between a scientific belief and a nonscientific one is that in the former there exists the possibility of demonstrating that it is false. If there is no way to demonstrate that an idea is false or even imagine such a demonstration, then you not only have an unscientific idea but a fanatical one, as well. Marxism, psychoanalysis, astrology, sensitivity training, and most forms of mysticism and superstition fall into this category. They are fanatical not because they are "false," but because they are frequently expressed in such a way that they can never be *shown* to be false. An astrologer can always "prove" that astrology is "correct." But what is the sort of evidence we may use to show that it is "incorrect"? Similarly, a Freudian analyst can always find evidence to confirm the essential correctness of his view. But if you ask him, what would you accept as evidence that your view is incorrect?, he has nothing to say. Psychoanalysis is a self-confirming system. The key to all fanatical beliefs is that they are self-confirming.

I grant that not all of our beliefs need to be put to such a rigorous test. We do not need to be "scientific" in every situation we are in. In many social contexts, for example, the function of our talk is not to say true things but to say pleasing things. Moreover, we sometimes must act *as if* a certain belief is infallible in order to get on with the business of living. To the extent that such a belief is *not* maladaptive, we are in no great danger. In a famous passage in a Sherlock Holmes story, the great observer and deductionist reveals to Watson that he does not know that the earth revolves around the sun. To Watson's astonishment, Holmes is completely indifferent to the matter, because, he points out, whichever way it is has no bearing on his life. We all have many such beliefs—whether they are false or not would make no great difference to the way in which we conduct ourselves. Problems arise when we must act in accordance with some belief, and when that action can have serious consequences. For example, Mr. and Mrs. Joseph Yourinko, of Absecom Heights, New Jersey, are Jehovah's Witnesses (or were at the time of this incident). Their young daughter, Linda Jean, was struck by a bus on her way to school. She was rushed to the hospital, where it was determined by surgeons that a blood transfusion was necessary to save her life. At that time, the law in New Jersey required parental permission in such cases, and her parents refused to give it on the ground that the Bible forbids the "eating of blood." Linda Jean died without ever regaining consciousness. It could be argued, of course, that the Yourinkos' concept of living was so constructed that, from their point of view, it was better to have a dead daughter than a live one who had "eaten" blood. Still, I would offer this as a classic example of fanaticism in action. The Yourinkos believed a certain sentence to be infallible. There was no possible way to demonstrate its falsity; that is, it is self-confirming. And it was, finally, maladaptive; it worked against the prospect of health and survival in a real situation.

Nonetheless, the Yourinkos appear odd only because, today, there are not many people who believe in the infallibility of the Bible. But this does not mean our store of infallible ideas is exhausted. The next time you go to a political rally of any kind (e.g., black liberation, gay liberation, union liberation, taxpayers' liberation), you will hear enough to keep your cup overflowing. In fact, the flow of "infallible" ideas is insured by the existence of many "systems" within our culture which claim to offer total and authoritative explanations of human affairs: Capitalism, Communism, Behaviorism, Catholicism, Feminism, Guruism, Billy Grahamism, Liberalism, Scientism. Such systems are not simply points of view from which hypotheses about "reality" are generated. For true believers, they consist largely of ideas that are not susceptible to testing of any sort, and, in fact, this untestability is perhaps the source of their appeal.

I can assure you that I am well aware that life is difficult, and that each of us can use all the help that is available in sorting things out. I must also tell you that I am not objecting to the "content" of the systems of belief I have referred to. For all I know, the assertions of Billy Graham or B. F. Skinner or Germaine Greer or the Bible are absolutely correct. Fanaticism resides not in the content of belief but in the process by which it is asserted. Our only protection from it lies in our will to refute.

The "true believer" syndrome requires some further comment, largely because it is so prevalent. My word for the problem is systemaphilia.

Systemaphilia arises from the assumption that human beings are sufficiently clever, knowledgeable, and multi-perspective to design complete and just about perfect systems of human activity. The much-admired Buckminster Fuller suffers from systemaphilia. So did Karl Marx, John Dewey, Rousseau, and Joseph Stalin. What these very different men had in common was a belief in the feasibility of total change. Having noticed that the purposes and structures of various human situations were faulty, indecent, or even depraved, they imagined systems which would in every respect be more desirable than those that existed. Systemaphiles are sometimes greatly praised for their efforts, and we express our admiration by calling them visionaries or prophets.

But I think it is worth pointing out that what they propose never works. At least, not in the way they have predicted. Propheteering is a very dangerous enterprise and has rarely been responsible for the unqualified improvement of life. In fact, where human incompetence, injustice, and misery have actually been reduced, the improvement has usually been the result of ad hoc, piecemeal, sometimes even accidental approaches rather than of some well-coordinated, comprehensive plan.

Why this is so is easy enough to figure out. Human beings are, of course, fallible. We make mistakes by the carload, and not because of bad intentions. We make them because we do not know enough or cannot see in more than one direction at a time. We cannot even remember our past clearly, let alone predict our future. And yet, systemaphiles do not usually take into account the virtual certainty of error in human calculations. They unfold their plans as if error were only an occasional defect in the edifice of human history, whereas Error is the name of the building itself. Second, if, indeed, humanity is making any "progress" at all, then it has come, and always comes, at great expense. Progress is a Faustian bargain, and not always a good one. For every step "forward," there is at least one step sideways and sometimes one or two back. To "get" progress, we must "unget" something of value. One of the more poignant expressions of this idea is found in *Inherit the Wind*, as Henry Drummond speaks to the jury:

Gentlemen, progress has never been a bargain. You've
got to pay for it. Sometimes I think there's a man behind
a counter who says, "All right, you can have a telephone;
but you'll have to give up privacy, the charm of distance.
Madam, you may vote; but at a price; you lose the right
to retreat behind a powder puff or a petticoat. Mister,
you may conquer the air; but the birds will lose their
wonder, and the clouds will smell of gasoline" ... Dar-
win moved us forward to a hilltop, where we could look
back and see the way from which we came. But for this
view, this insight, this knowledge, we must abandon our
faith in the pleasant poetry of genesis.

Systemaphiles do not like this kind of talk because it
threatens the purity of their systems. It implies a dark
side to what they propose, a contradiction. There is, of
course, something about a contradiction that no one
loves. But systemaphiles hate them most of all. You can
judge this for yourself the next time you hear or read
of a comprehensive proposal to redesign our transporta-
tion system or school system or political system or legal
system. What you will find missing from it are any prophecies about what will go wrong, what mistakes will be
made, or what negative consequences will arise from it.
These considerations are absent because systemaphiles
create plans based on oversimplified assumptions and
one-dimensional metaphors. In an effort to reduce a situation to a single set of clear principles, systemaphiles
have to ignore all paradoxes, contradictions, and competing principles. They have to overlook the possibilities
of error, and to pretend that nothing of value can be lost.
As Lewis Mumford points out: "Life cannot be reduced

to a system: the best wisdom, when so reduced to a single set of insistent notes, becomes a cacophony: indeed, the more stubbornly one adheres to a system, the more violence one does to life."

System-mongers, as Mumford calls them, seek to enforce acceptance by an entire community of some limiting principle and to design life in conformity to it. If life will not go along, then so much the worse for life. Which is, of course, crazy talk.

Role Fixation

How the religious faith in communication as panacea got started is mostly a mystery to me, but I suspect it is related to the development of the True Self industry, of which est, sensitivity training, and guruism are prosperous expressions. The basic assumption of this industry is that buried beneath your fumbling and miserable exterior is a True Self, which given half a chance will shine through and delight the world. For a fee, it can be helped to do so, and you may even learn how to be your own best friend in the bargain. A related assumption is that what the rest of us observe you doing all the time is merely a form of role-playing, which can and ought to be overcome by the irrepressible authenticity of your True Self. Apparently, it is possible to act like a grasping, lecherous, self-indulgent egocentric and still have a beautiful but invisible True Self. This belief can be very hard on those around you, but it is, of course, awfully good for business.

How your True Self got there, and what it is made of, is not clear, at least to me. I have been told that a man named Abraham Maslow knows, or once knew, but I have found his explanations mysterious. In any case, the True Self is obviously a metaphor and, therefore, cannot be either verified or refuted. But I think that at least as reasonable as postulating a True Self is to say that what we *are* is simply a composite of all the roles we know how to play well and comfortably. In other words, we do not have a Self, but a set of interconnected selves which we resourcefully call upon as we move from one situation to another. By *interconnected*, I mean to suggest that there is an obvious consistency in the way we tend to play out each of our roles—as daughter, lover, wife, mother, student, worker, friend, etc.—and it is this consistency to which we give the name "our character," or "identity." When someone says, "That's not like you," we are being told that our handling of a particular role does not match, in tone, point of view, vocabulary, etc., our handling of other roles with which our accuser is familiar. If someone wishes to call this consistency our True Self, I have no objection, but it is certainly not hidden from view. It is, in fact, the most visible thing about us.

Of course, one may have a particular way of handling a certain role—say, as lover—which is not open to public scrutiny and which, at the same time, is drastically different from the character of one's public performances. But there is no compelling reason to think of *that* self as being any more True than the selves the rest of us can observe.

I do not mean to imply that all selves are of equal

importance or prominence. To begin with, there is a self which seems to supervise our other selves. It is the quiet voice which tells us which self to call upon, and whether or not the right selection has been made. If we cannot get along without the idea of a True Self, then I nominate the supervisor-self for the post. It is the self to which we attach the name *our judgment* or *reason*. Then too, there are certain selves that simply play a more important part in the conduct of our lives than others. But the important point is that there is no such thing as a "private" self. Even the selves that take form only when no one else is around presuppose the existence of a social context (or a semantic environment). Walter Mitty presented one self to his wife and several others to his imagination. But even in his imaginings, he put himself in a social role—that is, in relation to other people. All selves are social roles which we either play or can imagine ourselves playing. And what Walter Mitty is famous for is nothing different from what all of us do: In our imaginations, we test ourselves in various roles. We practice saying this or that, and we invent replies from the people around us. Of course, if in reality we never have an opportunity to *do* a certain role, then it remains only a possibility, an unrealized self.

All selves, then, are called into existence by social context, as George Herbert Mead taught us. There is no existence, except as we exist *in* a situation. For all practical purposes, what we are is how we conduct ourselves in different environments, or how we can imagine conducting ourselves. Our conduct is, of course, predominantly language. And language always involves an act of prediction. Every time we say something, we are hypothesizing a certain kind of response from others. If our remark is intended to call forth a warm and gracious response, but instead produces cold rejection, our hypothesis has been refuted, and we must ask, Where does the trouble lie? To the extent that our language in a particular semantic environment produces consequences which we did not anticipate, we have a reason to suspect ourselves of stupid talk. In fact, stupid talk frequently comes from an inexperienced self, a self which cannot manage affairs well because it does not know enough about the situation which called it forth. But it is also a fascinating fact that some of us grow to love a certain self (i.e., a certain way of talking) to such an extent that we will use it in almost every semantic environment. This usually happens because in the situations where it *is* appropriate, it works for us, and works well. We feel competent in that role and, therefore, confident that we can control the situation. Our hypotheses about the responses of others are confirmed.

But we run into difficulty when we enter situations in which our favorite role is not appropriate. Where we hypothesize respect, we produce derision. Where we hypothesize sympathy, we produce hostility. Where we hypothesize agreement, we produce opposition. In Transactional Analysis, this situation is explained in the following way: Each of us has three basic roles, or selves—Adult, Parent, and Child. Each of these roles is characterized by a certain way of talking. The Adult, for example, tends to be descriptive and information-seeking; the Parent, prescriptive and authoritarian; the Child, helpless and demanding. Our transactions with others are satisfying to the extent that the role we are playing complements the role of another. If, for example, I am playing Parent to someone else's Child, things ought to work out pretty well. If, however, I am playing Adult to someone else's Child, then there is likely to be difficulty, since I cannot supply in that role what the other demands. I think this explanation is rather too streamlined a way to express the matter, since it reduces all possible selves to only three categories. It also focuses almost exclusively on one's relationship to others, and gives insufficient attention to the purposes of situations. People may have a satisfying transaction with each other but nonetheless fail to achieve more important ends. In other words, the appropriateness of one's role is determined not only by the character of those within the environment, but by the purposes of the environment as well. Transactional Analysis is, nonetheless, an extremely valuable construct. It helps us to see a) that we have different selves, b) that the environment we are in tells us which self we need to call upon, and c) that to be "stuck" on one self —a self for all reasons, as it were—leads to failure.

We all know people who cannot transit from one semantic environment to another. Professors, for instance, are apt to remain Professors even in situations where none are required. And there are Political People who see Significance in someone's ordering scrambled eggs. And there are Comics who are always "on." And Moralists for whom there is no joy anywhere, only responsibility. And Cynics who will never let themselves be awed, or let anything be revered. Such people may be said to be self- or role-fixated, and, what is worse, they are apt to assert their fixation as a virtue. They think of themselves as having a "strong character," but they may also be seen as people who are impoverished, single-dimensional, lacking at least the courage to try out new selves and so to grow.

And here I come as close to a definition of "health" as I can offer. For if health means anything, it is to grow. And growth implies both diversity and flexibility. Semantic health cannot be acquired through the mastery of some simple formula for a single way of talking, or some regimen for developing a perfect True Self. It is a measure of one's ability to move with competence through a wide range of semantic environments and with conviction through an equally wide range of social roles. And this requires intelligence, experience, and the courage to experiment with new selves. It does not mean that one must be all things to all people or have a self that is comfortable in every conceivable situation. There are purposes that ought not to be implemented, situations that should be subverted, and selves that must be rejected if we are to maintain that consistency we call our identity. Semantic flexibility has its limits. At one end of the continuum lies role-fixation, and stupid talk is its most characteristic symptom. At the other end lies schizophrenia, and crazy talk is its hallmark every time. But in between lies a wide range of opportunities for self-development and for its expression through talk that is effective, productive, and above all, sane.

The IFD Disease

The late and most esteemed Wendell Johnson coined this term, and I have always found it an apt name for a peculiar but prevalent kind of crazy talk. The *I* stands for idealization, the *F* for frustration, and the *D* for demoralization. Thus, the IFD disease is a process—a progression, if you will—from one state of mind to another. But it is a most unhappy progression, leaving you at the end in a very different place from where you expected to be. The trip begins, as with most things, with our talking to ourselves (or, as Johnson once put it as the title of one of his books, with talking to "your most enchanted listener"). Naturally, we want the best for our future, and so we set wonderful goals in life. We tell ourselves that we want to be "happy" or "successful" or "rich" or "fulfilled" or "at peace with ourselves." These seem to be reasonable goals, especially since there is so much reference to them in the culture, and so much advice on how to achieve them. But there is frequently a lethal flaw in such words. They are easy to summon but hard to define. In particular, they are hard to define operationally. That is, many people have no idea what situation would need to develop in life in order for them to be "happy" or "successful." Nor do they reflect on the question itself. All they know or want to know is that they are trying to be happy or successful or whatever. The word is an idealization, for which there are only the vaguest referents in reality, or none at all. What is happening, of course, is that such people are engaged in a dangerous search; for its object is only a word and not a situation. They begin their search full of hopes, but descend soon enough into frustration and eventually into despair. If you do not know what it will take to make you happy or successful, then you cannot know if that is what you have achieved.

Johnson and other counselors have reported on the small armies of people who have sought psychological help because they have been demoralized in their search for "real" success or peace or fulfillment. It is not enough that they are making a living, not enough that their children are healthy, not enough that they have a summer home or that their spouses are agreeable and loving people. Somehow, fulfillment and true happiness have eluded them. There is "something else," but they do not know what it looks like or where it is. Their words have become things which do not exist. This is, of course, a form of crazy talk, and its correction, as Johnson taught, lies in trying to connect your language with real and specific possibilities. Happiness, in other words, is a warm onion roll with cream cheese on it. Or, if your sights are loftier, it is being able to start your car in the morning when the

temperature is eight degrees. Or, if it is not that, at least
it must be something that you *do* or can imagine yourself
doing, something specific and achievable. Unless our
language is so grounded, we do not know where we have
landed, or if.

At the cultural level, the IFD disease is equally prevalent. At the moment, in America, there is a widespread
search being undertaken for our "moral fiber" and our
sense of "conviction and resolve." I would like to join in
the search, and I would do so, if someone would tell me
what the objects look like and how I will know when
they are found. In other words, what is it that Americans
must *do* (or not do) in order to claim victory over themselves. We read that Americans must "restore their faith
in the democratic process," which implies, of course, that
we have lost it. And yet, within the past several years,
one American President has declined to stand for office
because of a credibility gap. An American Vice President
has been turned out in disgrace. Another President re-
signed because the press uncovered certain of his "crimes,"
and the courts threw dozens of his associates in the slam-
mer. Through all of this, the transfer of power has been
orderly, and our present leaders are being carefully eval-
uated and criticized. Does this not reflect "faith" in the
democratic process? Is this not resolution and conviction
—and moral fiber, to boot? Perhaps not, but then what
would be?

I should say, finally, that in avoiding the IFD disease,
one does not have to avoid setting goals, even those that
would appear difficult to achieve. What Wendell Johnson was talking about is that the language of goal-setting
must be of this world, or else there is no goal.

Model Muddles

Let us suppose you have just finished being examined by a doctor. In pronouncing his verdict, he says somewhat accusingly, "Well, you've done a very nice case of arthritis here." You would undoubtedly think this is a strange diagnosis, or more likely, a strange doctor. People do not "do" arthritis. They "have" it, or "get" it, and it is a little insulting for the doctor to imply that you have produced or manufactured an illness of this kind, especially since arthritis will release you from certain obligations and, at the same time, elicit sympathy from other people. It is also painful. So the idea that you have done arthritis to yourself suggests a kind of self-serving masochism.

Now, let us suppose a judge is about to pass sentence on a man convicted of robbing three banks. The judge advises him to go to a hospital for treatment, saying with an air of resignation, "You certainly have a bad case of criminality." On the face of it, another strange remark.

People do not "have" criminality. They "do" crimes, and we are usually outraged, not saddened, by their "doings." At least that is the way we are accustomed to thinking about the matter.

The point I am trying to make is that such simple verbs as "is" or "does" are, in fact, powerful metaphors which express some of our most fundamental conceptions of the way things are. We believe, for example, that there are certain things that people "have," and certain things that people "do," and even certain things that people "are." These beliefs do not necessarily reflect the structure of reality. They simply reflect a traditional way of talking about reality. In his book *Erewhon*, Samuel Butler depicted a society that lives according to the metaphors of my strange doctor and strange judge. There, illness is something people "do" and therefore have moral responsibility for; criminality is something you "have" and therefore is quite beyond your control. Every legal system and every moral code is based on a set of assumptions about what people "are," "have," or "do." And, I might add, any significant changes in law or morality are preceded by a reordering of how such metaphors are employed.

I am not, incidentally, recommending the culture of Erewhon. I am only trying to highlight the fact that there is a certain measure of arbitrariness to our ideas. And to the degree that we are unaware of how our own ways of talking put such ideas in our heads, we are not in the fullest control of our situation.

In schools, for instance, we find that tests are given to determine how smart someone is or, more precisely, how much smartness someone "has." If one child scores a 138, and another a 106, the first is thought to "have" more smartness than the other. But this seems to me a strange conception—every bit as strange as "doing" arthritis or "having" criminality. I do not know anyone who *has* smartness. The people I know sometimes *do* smart things (as far as I can judge) and sometimes *do* stupid things—depending on what circumstances they are in, and how much they know about a situation, and how interested they are. "Smartness," so it seems to me, is a specific performance, done in a particular set of circumstances. It is not something you *are* or have in measurable quantities. In fact, the assumption that smartness is something you *have* has led to such nonsensical ideas as "over-" and "underachievers." As I understand it, an overachiever is someone who doesn't *have* much smartness but does a lot of smart things. An underachiever is someone who *has* a lot of smartness but does a lot of stupid things.

In any case, I am not prepared here to argue the matter through. Although I have not heard of them, there may be good reasons to imagine that smartness or honesty or sensitivity are "qualities" that people *have* in measurable proportions and that exist independently of what people actually do. What I am driving at is this: All language is metaphorical, and often in the subtlest ways. In the simplest sentence, sometimes in the simplest word, we do more than merely express ourselves. We construct reality along certain lines. We make the world according to our own imagery. Consider, for example, a straightforward question, such as, "Do you see the point I am trying to make?" Why *see* the point? And why a *point*? Is an idea something you can see? Is it something that converges, or drives a wedge, or indicates a direction? Can an idea fade from view? Can it illuminate a problem? Can someone's ideas jump around from place to place? Can they be marched forward in an orderly fashion? What is an "idea" anyway—a point, a light bulb, a jumping bean, a regiment? Well, ideas are all of these things, and anything else we wish to make them, depending, I suppose, on how we construe the "mind." Is the mind a dark cavern, which is illuminated by ideas? Is it a vessel, which is filled by ideas? Or is it a muscle which may be strengthened? Or a garden to be cultivated? Or a shapeless piece of clay that may be carefully molded?

Obviously, there is no answer to these questions. I raise them to make plausible the idea that language is a design for living. To talk is to imagine a world of make-believe, to hypothesize that everything is like something else. A molecule is like a billiard ball, and a billiard ball is like a planet, and a planet is like a speeding rocket, and a rocket is like a bird, and a bird is like a leaf floating in the wind. Of course, our best poets and scientists are those who have created the most vivid and enduring metaphors: The Lord is my shepherd; life is a stage; the universe is a great clock; the mind is a seething cauldron of emotions covered over with a thin coating of civilization. In poetry and science, such metaphors are usually called to our attention. They are, in fact, forced on our awareness by being placed at the center of what we are to consider, and they may be rigorously examined. But in everyday speech situations, we are apt to be unaware of how we are using our metaphors, and therein lies a source of considerable confusion.

To begin with, in discussing the difficulties that our metaphors pose, I do not have in mind anything of the sort that English teachers usually worry about. For instance, I do not believe that "mixing" our metaphors is a great burden on human communication. It is all right with me if William Shakespeare wants Hamlet to "take arms against a sea of troubles," or if anyone else wants us to "run a tight ship while on the road to freedom" (as I once heard a politician say). There is, to be sure, a certain impreciseness, if not a little absurdity, in a muddled image, but it is not the stuff of which serious human problems are made. Nor do I feel that the absence of vivid metaphors in our speech or the excessive use of clichés ("dead as a doornail") will generate insurmountable difficulties. These are all matters of personal style whose worst consequence will be a certain tiresomeness. What I am talking about, as always, is a semantic environment, and in particular, the way in which a situation takes on the aspect of something else.

It frequently happens (in fact all the time) that people within a particular semantic environment will construe the situation in entirely different ways; that is, each constructs a different mètaphor for what is happening. For example, I have observed that some people, upon entering a bank, will conduct themselves as if they were in a cathedral. Everything about their demeanor suggests that, from their point of view, there is something holy about the place and the transactions that occur there. It would not surprise me to know that there are people who, inside a bank, summon exactly the same emotions they call upon when attending a Sunday service.

Of course, people who work in banks are apt to construe the situation as something entirely different—let us say, for instance, a department store. Now, if one man thinks he is in a department store, and another man thinks he is in a church, their interaction will be exceedingly curious, and the former will have a heavy advantage over the latter.

That is why bank executives go to such lengths to create and maintain an atmosphere of sanctity in their banks. This is achieved through the bank's architecture, its interior design, the clothing and uniforms worn, and the language used. No one, for example, talks loudly. When people converse with the tellers, they speak as if they were sharing a confidence—even making a confession of some sort. One bank I know very well provides organ music throughout the day. And once I had the rare privilege of being there when the main vault was opened. The scene —including the responses of the "customers"—reminded me of nothing so much as the opening of the Ark to remove the Torah. It is an unusual person indeed who can think of himself as a "customer" in relation to a bank. Which is fine, I am sure, with bank executives. Banks surely do not want "customers." Nor do they want "friends." They prefer "supplicants," perhaps "defendants," possibly "patients"— in short, any construction of the situation which will foster a sense of awe, rather than curiosity, aggressiveness, or ease.

Doctors present a similar situation. Who can enter a doctor's office or a hospital and construe his or her role in the situation as that of a "customer"? Many people I know are apt to think of themselves, when sitting in a doctor's office, as a student who has been called upon to explain some difficulty to the principal. Such "patient-students" are reluctant to take too much of the "doctor-principal's" time, they do not address him by his first name, they do not ask questions, they are eager to do exactly as they are told, and if the doctor tells them that he can see nothing wrong with the ear of which they have complained, they are apologetic about having mentioned it in the first place.

Doctors, of course, go to expensive lengths to generate and sustain such a metaphor. Their offices, for example, are designed to create exactly the same sense of mystery, anxiety, and guilt that a school principal's office invariably does. You are summoned when the *doctor* is ready, not when *you* are. And if the doctor summons you one hour and twenty minutes later than your appointment called for, he does not apologize. Why should he? If you had not screwed up in the first place, you wouldn't be there. Then, too, the doctor's decisions are, like a principal's, always mysterious, or at least vaguely arbitrary. From a student's point of view, staying after school is a punishment that bears about the same relation to the nature of his offense as a "G.I." series does to the nature of the patient's "offense." You submit to it because you have been told you must. But it is never quite clear as to how you will be improved by the procedure.

What happens in a bank or a doctor's office is not different from what happens anyplace else: Every semantic environment is projected as being something other than it is. This is no mental aberration. Metaphorizing is the principal means by which we think. The process is roughly the same for all of us, although the content will vary from individual to individual. To one man, the army is a prison. To another, it is an organized religion. To a third, it is a sporting event. To one teacher, the classroom is a criminal court. To another, it is a projection of his own home. And to a third, it is an institute for working through his own psychological problems. Naturally, what we have construed a situation to be will determine how we will conduct ourselves. The teacher who thinks he is in a psychiatrist's office when he enters a classroom feels, says, and does different things from one who thinks he is a judge or a surrogate parent or a top sergeant or a stand-up comic. That is obvious enough, and individual differences in metaphor projection need not be a problem except under certain conditions.

As I mentioned before, the first and most obvious of these conditions is when two or more people within a semantic environment have constructed different and incompatible metaphors of the situation, and are largely unaware of what is happening. For instance, in marriage it frequently happens that the male "partner" (an interesting metaphor in itself) construes the situation as his fiefdom, his home being his castle, and his wife and children being vassals subject to his authority. There is no problem here if wife and children construe the situation in a similar way. After all, feudalism worked tolerably well for centuries. In any case, where two people function within the same metaphorical framework, there is a minimum of conflict, and I suppose that is what Eric Berne means by a "complementary relationship." But if the wife construes the situation, let us say, as a capitalist enterprise, with enlightened self-interest as a central idea, her behavior will frequently appear unreasonable to her husband, and his, in turn, unreasonable to her. Not all conflict, of course, is traceable to incompatible metaphors, but it is useful to assume that much of it can be. By *incompatible*, I mean two metaphors whose implied roles and rules are so incongruent that the "reasonable" actions of one person will inevitably conflict with the "reasonable" actions of another. The doctor who thinks of his profession as a priestly craft will naturally think his "parishioners" arrogant if they ask too many questions or seek to penetrate the mysteries of his ministrations. The patient who thinks of himself as a "customer" will naturally think of the doctor as an arrogant businessman who has insufficient respect for those on whom his income is dependent. Both seek a good relationship, but they will not achieve it.

A problem may also arise when someone constructs a metaphor whose configuration nowhere coincides with the realities of any actual situation in which he finds himself. The technical name for such a process is paranoia. Mental hospitals are a good place (although not the only one) to find people who have constructed metaphors which bear no relationship to any possible situation. For example, people who imagine they are saviors, czars, spies, or movie stars. Their problem is not that *they* think they are such exalted personages, but that other people do not. You are "crazy" only when nothing and no one in your environment will lend support to the metaphor you have constructed for yourself. If, however, you are in a situation where other people are willing to act as if your metaphor is plausible, you are quite "normal." For example, the late Gen. George Patton apparently believed, with as much sincerity as your average lunatic, that in a previous life he had been a commander of some sort in the Roman legions. Since this belief did not hinder him in his work—in fact, added something to it—and since few people he came into contact with were in a position to dispute it, Patton is usually thought of as a national hero.

There are differences, of course, between people who believe they *are* an emperor and those who merely act *as if* they are. The main difference being that the former will always perform as an emperor while the latter will do so only when the environment assists in sustaining the performance. Which leads to still another problem with our metaphors. There are some of us who tend to become fixated on certain metaphors. Our problem is not that we have obliterated the distinction between metaphor and reality, but that we cannot seem to generate a rich enough mixture of metaphors with which to interpret reality. For example, some people see almost every situation as a contest in which they are players. Their object, naturally, is to "win" or at least to avoid "losing." There is no doubt that in many situations—politics, for instance, or business—such a metaphor is useful in helping people achieve their purposes. There is, after all, a certain structural correspondence between the rules of a game and the rules of politics and business.

But the metaphor becomes ludicrous when it forms the basis of relationships in, for example, love-making, praying, learning, or caring for one's health. The patient who, upon being asked by his dentist which tooth troubled him, replied, "You're the dentist, *you* tell me," is using an adversary (contest) metaphor which will do neither him nor the dentist any good. The automobile driver who is insulted by being passed on the road, and the student who will beat his teacher out of an A without having done any of the work "personally" are perhaps more realistic examples of someone's projecting a "game" metaphor onto a situation that calls for something quite different. Why people get stuck within the boundaries of a single and a singularly inappropriate metaphor is difficult to say. Sometimes, no doubt, it has to do with the circumstances of our upbringing. You may call it one's "life script," if you will, but the point is that to some people "life is no picnic, it's a struggle, a battle, a game with winners and losers." From this metaphorical premise, all the subenvironments which comprise "life" are viewed as varying forms of competition: marriage, education, friendships, religion, etc.

But sometimes our inability to choose from a variety of possible metaphors has to do with the fact that someone else in an environment has forced us to accept his or her metaphorical construction. Take the case, for example, of a student who finds himself in a situation where everyone else—administrators, his teachers, his parents, admissions officers—construes school as a competition. (You know the joke, I'm sure, about the student who proudly shows his father a test paper on which he received a 97. The father says, "Who got the other three points?") In order to survive in such an environment, the student must view matters as they do. There are environments, however, in which an individual, being aware of the metaphor controlling the situation and wishing to change it, can be effective. "If patients want doctors to stop acting like God," I have heard a doctor say, "then they must get off their knees." In other words, a certain measure of compliance is required to make a metaphor work. If you refuse to be a contestant or a recalcitrant child or a supplicant or whatever is demanded, you can (sometimes) force everyone in a situation to reconstruct it along more suitable lines.

In summary, then, we may say that every semantic environment is controlled by metaphors, frequently hidden from the view of those who have created them, but through which people interpret the meaning and value of what is happening. Where people have a roughly similar construction of a situation—whether they see themselves in a prison, in a race, in a hospital, in a court of law, in a church, or whatever—the environment will function with a minimum of disruption. Serious difficulties arise, however, when people's metaphors clash, and especially when there is a lack of awareness of how the metaphors are controlling their responses. I might add in this connection that such clashes and lack of awareness are as prevalent in academic and professional communities as anywhere else. For instance, in the extraordinary book *Models of Madness, Models of Medicine*, by Miriam Siegler and Humphry Osmond, there is an excellent depiction of the current confusion in the psychiatric profession over the question Which metaphor ought to be used for madness? Is madness a disease (the medical model)? Is it a character defect (the moral model)? Is it the result of a "sick" society (the social model)? Is it a mind-expanding trip (the psychedelic model)? Does it exist only in the eye of the beholder (the conspiratorial model)? And so on. Such a "model muddle" is common enough in many academic disciplines (especially in the field of communication), and to the extent that scholars are aware of the problem, such a situation can be stimulating and productive. After all, each metaphor invites an entirely different view of a matter and as a result may increase one's understanding of the multifaceted richness of an issue. However, where there is a minimum of awareness of different metaphorical premises, confusion, impotence, and bad temper are the usual consequences, as is the case with all semantic environments in which people do not know that they are faced with a serious model muddle.

It remains for me to address the question How can we determine what someone's controlling metaphor is in any situation? To answer this question, one must pay attention to a large number of factors, including body language, clothing, and the ways in which people design the physical environments in which they function (assuming they have some control over them). But largely, you may uncover your own metaphors, as well as those of another, by attending to language. No one is entirely consistent in his or her use of metaphors, but most of us have a characteristic metaphorical content for each of the situations we are in. For instance, one teacher I know has obviously construed his classroom to be a military situation of some sort. He calls his students his "troops," and they are forever "attacking" problems. When students are absent, they are "AWOL," and he and his troops together are in a "war" against ignorance. I am not implying, incidentally, that this metaphor is necessarily inappropriate. His students appear to accept it and not only cover a lot of territory but advance on all fronts.

Many businessmen, I have noticed, are equally consistent in their development of another metaphor—people as machines. In these situations, people have "outputs," organizations "break down," "feedback" is sought after, and the office gets to "really humming." There has arisen considerable difficulty with this metaphor, because workers, having become increasingly aware of it, do not care for some of its implications. But that is another matter. What I am saying is that by noticing patterns of speech, including our own, we may get our best evidence as to how a situation has been construed, by ourselves or anyone else.

Reification

Reification means confusing words with things. In some ways, it is our most seductive source of stupid and crazy talk, since its origins are deeply embedded in the structure of language itself. The principal grammatical instrument through which reification is accomplished is the verb *to be* and its various forms. And since this verb comprises about one-third of all the verbs used in normal English discourse, we are all in constant danger of being afflicted. Here, for example, is a common type of reification, from the pen of William Safire of *The New York Times*:

> ... we should set aside the temptation to bedeck murderers with the verbal garland of "guerrilla" or "commando" or even "revolutionary." A person who kills another human being in a bank holdup, whether in the name of Basque separatism or Symbionese Liberation, is a murderer. ...

What Mr. Safire seems to be saying is that a person who kills another in a bank holdup might be *called* a guerrilla or a commando (by wrong-thinking people), but his "real" name *is* murderer. Here is a similar venture in reification by a letter-writer to the New York *Post*:

> The Post is inaccurate and misleading in using the word "radical" in describing Patty Hearst, the SLA, and Sara Moore. These are not "radicals" but are perhaps nihilists, crackpots, or militant revolutionaries.

This writer is not quite as sure as is Mr. Safire about what Patty Hearst's "real" name is, but he is very sure of what her real name is not. Certainly, we can assume that both writers would find the world a better place if only people would use the real names of things instead of verbal garlands and other fake, inaccurate, and misleading names.

The question arises, What do we mean by a real name? The answer is that there is no such thing. Our belief in real names originates in a kind of semantic illusion, sometimes referred to as the principle of identity. One of mankind's deepest intuitions is to respond to the symbols he invents as if they "are" whatever it is that he invented them to symbolize. In some "primitive" cultures one's "real name" is kept secret, because it is believed that knowing a person's name carries with it the power to control him. In "civilized" cultures, we know better, but not much. When we say that someone *is* something—a murderer, a nihilist, a crackpot, an enemy, a hero, or even Al Schwartz, we have the strongest feeling that this is not merely a name we are *calling* him, but that it *is* his name. It is inseparable from him. It is identical with him. What some people might call him is one thing; what he *is* is another. And so, with a few variations, people from all kinds of cultures invest names with an almost magical dimension.

From one point of view, all of this is utter nonsense. There are things and processes in the world, and then there are our names for them. Nothing could be simpler to understand—yet harder to remember. Communication depends on our agreeing to call things by the same name, but in supposing that a thing and its name are inherently, immutably linked, we are often led into committing acts of monumental and irreversible stupidity. The tragedy of Ibrahim, the Egyptian soldier shot by his comrades, is a case in point. There is a vast difference in how people behave when they are told, "one who does not know the password *is* the enemy," and when they are told, "for the purposes of this situation, we will use the name 'enemy' for those who do not know the password." The latter helps to remind us of the special purposes for which we have chosen a name; it reminds us that *we* have chosen the name, and that we may choose another as circumstances require. It reminds us, in short, that a name is a conscious act of human ingenuity, not an act of nature. Without this sort of understanding, we can block ourselves from knowing exactly what we and others are talking about. Mr. Safire, for example, is pulling the wool over our eyes, and possibly his own, in the remarks I have quoted. The only nonstupid translation I can make of his statement is as follows: By using the names *guerrillas*, *commandos*, or *revolutionaries* to refer to people who kill others in a bank holdup, we are accepting *their* construction of the meaning of the event. Such names imply heroism, dedication, a striving for political freedom. But if we use the name *murderers*, we may define the event differently and arrange our attitudes accordingly. In using the name *murderers*, we reject the relevance of political motivation, and we set aside any considerations of heroism or dedication. And so, Mr. Safire is saying, I want you to use *my* word, not theirs, because I want you to see these events the way I do.

So that my own bias is clear, let me tell you that I accept Mr. Safire's name, *murderers*, but in doing so, I fully understand that I am expressing my own political and sociological constructs and do not, for a moment, believe that "murderers" are what these people "really are." Mr. Safire, however, by implying that "murderers" is what they "really are," blurs our understanding of what he is asking us to do. For in the guise of telling us what is "real," he is only telling us what he believes to be politically desirable. This might be seen a bit more clearly by Mr. Safire if I could get him to read the following paragraph which I have just made up:

> We should set aside the temptation to bedeck murderers with the verbal garland of "air force personnel" or "bombardier" or "twice-decorated hero." A person who kills another human being in a bombing attack, whether in the name of "the domino theory" or "capitalism," is a murderer. . . .

I think Mr. Safire would object to this. He might say, "But a bombardier is not a murderer." To which I would say, "A bombardier *isn't* anything. He may be called a *murderer* or a *hero*, depending on what the name-caller wishes us to feel or to see." In other words, Mr. Safire is asking us to see and evaluate events from the perspective of his sociological construct. That is all there is to it. But it is difficult to know this from the manner in which he has expressed himself.

Of course, when it comes right down to it, what I am talking about is a concept of definition. People who believe that a name is identical with that which it names will also believe that words have "real" definitions. "What does —————— mean?" is the usual way we ask for a definition. The very form of the question is responsible, I believe, "for the peculiar paralysis [to quote I. A. Richards] that the mention and discussion of definitions induce." Apparently, it is extremely difficult for some people to grasp that a definition is not a manifestation of nature but an *instrument* for helping us to achieve our purposes. To quote Richards again: "We want to do something, and a definition is a means of doing it. If we want certain results, then we must use certain meanings (or definitions). But no definition has any authority apart from a purpose, or to bar us from other purposes."

This quote is, of course, a definition of definition, and you are entirely free to reject it. But consider that Richards, in defining a definition in this way, is trying to show us that our meanings are inseparable from our purposes, and that the idea of a "real" meaning is a snare and a delusion. His definition, in fact, is putting forward a different sort of question from the one we are accustomed to asking. Richards is suggesting that whenever someone defines a word or state of affairs, we are obliged to ask, not "Is he correct or incorrect?" but rather, "What purpose is served by his using this definition?" If William Safire wishes to define an "urban guerrilla" as a "murderer," that is his privilege. And if Patty Hearst wishes to define a "bombardier" as a "murderer," that is *her* privilege. *Our* responsibility is to determine what they hope to gain (from us) by doing so.

All of this makes understanding each other rather more complicated than we would wish. If only there were someplace where the true and real definitions of our words could be found, we could go there, study, and return, confident that we are right in the way we use our words. But there isn't. So we are left with what *I* call things, and with what *you* call things, and we live in hope that we can find people to talk to who call things by our names for them. Of course, we hope that in simple matters, there will be a high degree of naming-agreement, even among people whose psychological or political or sociological biases are quite different. A cigarette ought to be called a cigarette by anybody. And Saturday ought to be called Saturday and not Monday. And December 30 ought to be called December 30, or how can we get on with life? Well, even in these matters, we might well pause for reflection, as the following edict from the Prague government will suggest:

> Because Christmas Eve falls on a Thursday, the day has been designated a Saturday for work purposes. Factories will close all day, with stores open a half day only. Friday, December 25, has been designated a Sunday, with both factories and stores open all day. Monday, December 28, will be a Wednesday for work purposes. Wednesday, December 30, will be a business Friday. Saturday, January 2, will be a Sunday, and Sunday, January 3, will be a Monday.

One of the reasons this is so hilarious is that it gives us a glimpse of what things will be like when the world starts, finally, to go completely mad. It shows us a semantic environment starting to come unglued, for without some reasonable stability to meanings, our fundamental notions of what is reality become too fluid to be usable. And yet, there is (from my point of view) something admirable about this ridiculous attempt at redefinition by fiat. It is an example of people trying to master their own symbols rather than be mastered by them. The opposite of this edict is the case of the calendar reform which took place in 1752. In order to realign the calendar to coincide with the astronomical facts, the British government decreed that September 2 would henceforth be September 14. This decree was followed by a great hue and cry from the public, which held that such a change would deprive everyone of 11 days of their lives! *That* is an example of stupid talk, not unlike the reasoning of the person who, upon being told that the thermometer outside the window read 98 degrees, remarked, "No wonder it's so hot!" Or the person who thinks that pigs are called pigs because they are so dirty. Or the person who thinks that murderers are murderers because they are murderers.

To reify words is to invest them with sacredness and, therefore, to reverse the relationship that they may reasonably be assumed to have with "reality." In some semantic environments, this reversal is at the core of the system. In many religions, for example, symbols are assumed to *be* that which they stand for. To the Jews, the name of God may not be written. To the Christians, a wafer does not symbolize the body of Christ; it *is* the body. To the Hindus, a cow does not represent a sacred idea; it *is* the idea. In the face of this, I do not speak unconditionally against reification. It well may be that it is the basis of all sacredness in life, and in some respects, the world surely does not suffer from an excess of sacredness. For where there is little sacredness, there is also very little order. But in other respects, the world *does* suffer from an excess of sacredness—a greater devotion to words than to the realities they refer to. People kill over words, over how things should be described. He who does not have my word is my enemy.

And so, in the end, reification is a blessing and a curse. Through it, we gain a certain measure of control over the world of things, for if we have the word, we have the thing (or so we suppose). But in so supposing, we may make ourselves stupid and then crazy. Unless, of course, we know we are only supposing.

Silent Questions

I cannot vouch for the story, but I have been told that once upon a time, in a village in what is now Lithuania, there arose a most unusual problem. A curious disease afflicted many of the townspeople. It was mostly fatal (although not always), and its onset was signaled by the victim's lapsing into a deathlike coma. Medical science not being quite so advanced as it is now, there was no definite way of knowing if the victim was actually dead when it appeared seemly to bury him. As a result, the townspeople feared that several of their relatives had already been buried alive and that a similar fate might await them —a terrifying prospect, and not only in Lithuania. How to overcome this uncertainty was their dilemma.

One group of people suggested that the coffins be well stocked with water and food and that a small air vent be drilled into them just in case one of the "dead" happened to be alive. This was expensive to do, but seemed more than worth the trouble. A second group, however, came up with an inexpensive and more efficient idea. Each coffin would have a twelve-inch stake affixed to the inside of the coffin lid, exactly at the level of the heart. Then, when the coffin was closed, all uncertainty would cease.

There is no record as to which solution was chosen, but for my purposes, whichever it was is irrelevant. What is mostly important here is that the two different solutions were generated by two different questions. The first solution was an answer to the question, How can we make sure that we do not bury people who are still alive? The second was an answer to the question, How can we make sure that everyone we bury is dead?

The point is that all the answers we ever get are responses to questions. The questions may not be evident to us, especially in everyday affairs, but they are there nonetheless, doing their work. Their work, of course, is to design the form that our knowledge will take and therefore to determine the direction of our actions. A great deal of stupid and/or crazy talk is produced by bad, unacknowledged questions which inevitably produce bad and all-too-visible answers.

As far as I can determine, there are at least four important reasons why question-asking language causes us problems. The first is that our questions are sometimes formed at such a high level of abstraction that we cannot answer them at all. "Why am I a failure?" and "What is the meaning of life?" are typical examples. The connection between a question of this form and the "IFD disease" is fairly obvious: The key words in the questions are so vague that it is a mystery to know where to begin looking for answers. For example, in trying to respond helpfully to a troubled questioner who asks, Why am I a failure?, a sensible person would have to ask several more pointed questions to get within answering range: What do you mean by "failure"? What specifically have you "failed" at? When have these "failures" taken place? In what circumstances? What do you mean by "success," when and where have you experienced it, and how many "successes" have you had? What needs to be done with such questions is to "operationalize" them, to restate them in forms that will allow for concrete, reality-oriented answers. In the process of doing this, one may discover that the question being asked was not so much, "Why am I a failure?" but, "Why did my marriage end in divorce?" "Why did I lose my job?" or even something as relatively simple as, "Why did I fail advanced calculus?"

I do not say that questions about one's dead marriage or lost job are easy ones; only that they are more approachable than loose-ended questions that imply one's nature is marred by some nondefinable affliction called *failure*.

It is characteristic of the talk of troubled people that they will resist bringing their questions down to a level of answerability. If fanaticism is falling in love with an irrefutable answer, then a neurosis is falling in love with an unanswerable question. "Why are people always trying to cheat me?" or "When will the breaks start to come my way?" is the sort of question that can be treacherously endearing. As it stands, there is no answer to it, and perhaps that is why some people choose to ask it and ask it repeatedly. It is, in fact, not so much a question as a kind of assertion that the responsibility for one's life lies entirely outside oneself. But because it has the *form* of a question, one may well be deceived into trying to answer it, which will lead to continuous frustration and demoralization.

Of course, questions of this type are not confined to one's personal relationship to the cosmos but are also used, unfortunately, as an instrument for discovering "facts." And they produce the same unsatisfying results. "Who is the best President that America has ever had?" is the sort of commonplace, completely unanswerable question which results in no knowledge at all. The conversation between Stupid Talk and Sensible Talk usually goes something like this:

> *Stupid Talk*: Who's the best President we ever had?
>
> *Sensible Talk*: What do you mean by "best"?
>
> *Stupid Talk*: What do you mean "What do I mean?"? Best means "the best," "the most excellent," "tops."
>
> *Sensible Talk*: "Tops" in what respect? Most votes? Least criticized? Most well-read? Richest?
>
> *Stupid Talk*: What do those things have to do with it? I mean "the best"—all around.
>
> *Sensible Talk*: Using what criteria for which aspects of his performance?
>
> *Stupid Talk*: Why are you making this so complicated? You mean to tell me you don't know what "best" means?
>
> *Sensible Talk*: Right.
>
> *Stupid Talk*: Jeez!

Now, it is possible I am being unfair to Stupid Talk here, in that he may have asked the question only in order to get some diversion at a rather dull party. If that was his intention, then you should reverse the names of the characters in my scene. Sensible Talk is simply being obnoxious or has misunderstood the purpose of the semantic environ-

ment he is in. But if the question was asked to start a serious conversation, resulting in the development and expression of informed opinion, then the names of my characters
must stand as they are. The question as originally posed
will not produce a discussable answer. I might add, as
well, that even a seemingly specific question, such as Who
discovered oxygen?, is unanswerable except insofar as it
implies a somewhat longer and more detailed question.
For example, if the question means to say, "According to
the *Encyclopaedia Britannica*, who is credited with the
discovery of oxygen?," it is certainly answerable. But that
is really quite a different question from "Who discovered
oxygen?" and the difference, I would insist, is not "mere
semantics." I have not verified it, but my guess is that textbooks in the Soviet Union do not credit Joseph Priestley
and Karl Wilhelm Scheele with discovering oxygen and
may not even credit Lavoisier with coining the word. I do
not say "they" are right and "we" are wrong. But in such
matters as who did what and when, there are always lively
and even legitimate disputes, and if you do not take into
account *in your question* the source of the knowledge you
are seeking, there is bound to be trouble.

The first problem, then, in question-asking language
may be stated in this way: The type of words used in a
question will determine the type of words used in the answer. In particular, question-words that are vague, subjective, and not rooted in any verifiable reality will produce
their own kind in the answer.

A second problem arises from certain structural characteristics, or grammatical properties, of sentences. For example, many questions seem almost naturally to imply
either-or alternatives. "Is that good?" (as against "bad"),

"Is she smart?" (as against "dumb"), "Is he rich?" (as against "poor"), and so on. The English language is heavily biased toward "either-or-ness," which is to say that it encourages us to talk about the world in polarities. We are inclined to think of things in terms of their singular opposites rather than as part of a continuum of multiple alternatives. *Black* makes us think of *white*, *rich* of *poor*, *smart* of *dumb*, *fast* of *slow*, and so on. Naturally, when questions are put in either-or terms, they will tend to call forth an either-or answer. "This is bad," "She's dumb," "He's poor," etc. There are many situations in which such an emphatic answer is all that is necessary, since the questioner is merely seeking some handy label, to get a "fix" on someone, so to speak. But, surprisingly and unfortunately, this form of question is also used in situations where one would expect a more serious and comprehensive approach to a subject. For example, in Edwin Newman's popular book, *Strictly Speaking*, he asks in his subtitle, "Will America Be the Death of English?" The form of the question demands either a *yes* or a *no* for its answer. (Newman, by the way, says yes, and for no particular reason, so far as I could tell.) Had the question been phrased as, "To what extent will English be harmed (impoverished, diminished, etc.) by Americans?" you would have had a very boring subtitle but, in my opinion, a much more serious book, or at least the possibility of one. Questions which ask, "To what extent" or "In what manner" invite a more detailed, qualified look at a problem than questions which ask, "Is it this or that?" The latter divide the universe into two possibilities; the former allow one to consider the multiple possibilities inherent in a problem. "Is America an imperial power?" "Have we lost our faith in democracy?"

"Are our taxes too high?"—these are some questions which insinuate that a position must be taken; they do not ask that thought be given.

A similar structural problem in our questions is that we are apt to use singular forms instead of plural ones. What is the cause of . . . ? What is the reason for . . . ? What is the result of . . . ? As with either-or questions, the form of these questions limits our search for answers and therefore impoverishes our perceptions. We are not looking for causes, reasons, or results, but for *the* cause, *the* reason, and *the* result. The idea of multiple causality is certainly not unfamiliar, and yet the form in which we habitually ask some of our most important questions tends to discourage our thinking about it: What is the reason we don't get along? What is the cause of your overeating? What will be the effect of school integration? What is the problem that we face? I do not say that a question of this sort rules out the possibility of our widening our inquiries. But to the extent that we allow the form of such questions to go unchallenged, we are in danger of producing shallow and unnecessarily restricted answers.

This is equally true of the third source of problems in question-asking language, namely, the assumptions that underlie it. Unless we are paying very close attention, we can be led into accepting as fact the most precarious and even preposterous ideas. Perhaps the two most famous assumption-riddled questions are, Have you stopped beating your wife? and How many angels can dance on the head of a pin? But in almost every question, there lurks at least one assumption which may slip by if we are not accustomed to looking for it. By an assumption, I mean a belief that is not subject to scrutiny because it is so deeply embedded in the question that we are hardly even aware of its presence. Consider, for instance, such questions as these, which I have recently heard discussed on television: Why is America losing its moral direction? When will we achieve equality of opportunity? How does the white power structure operate? The first question assumes that there is such a thing as a "moral direction," that a country can have one, that America once did, and, of course, that we are presently losing it. I do not say that these assumptions are untenable, but each one of them is surely worth inquiring into before proceeding to the question. In fact, once you start discussing these assumptions, you may never get back to the original question, and may even find it has disappeared, to everyone's relief.

The second question assumes that there is such a thing as equality of opportunity; that it is, in some sense, "achievable" by society; that it is worth achieving; and that some effort is being made to achieve it—all extremely arguable assumptions in my opinion. I have, for example, long suspected that the phrase "equality of opportunity" is a kind of semantic fiction, not unlike the legal term "a reasonable and prudent man"; that is to say, one is free to give it almost any meaning that suits one's purpose in a given situation. In any case, I should want the term carefully defined before listening to a discussion of when "it" will be achieved.

The third question, of course, assumes the existence of a white power structure, as well as mechanisms through which it operates. Given the rather bumbling, haphazard ways of American business and government, I am inclined to be at least suspicious of this assumption, although I would like to hear it defended.

The point is that if you proceed to answer questions without reviewing the assumptions implicit in them, you may end up in never-never land without quite knowing how you got there. My favorite invitation to never-never land, incidentally, was extended to me by a young woman who asked, "Why do you think the extraterrestrials are coming in such large numbers to Earth?" You might expect that a person who would ask such a question also would have an answer to it—which was, you will be happy to know, "to help Earth people develop an effective World Organization."

The fourth source of difficulty in question-asking language is that two people in the same semantic environment may ask different questions about a situation, but without knowing it. For example, in a classroom, the teacher may be asking himself, "How can I get the students to learn this?" But it is almost certain that the students are asking, "How can I get a good grade in this course?" Naturally, two different questions will generate two different approaches to the situation and may be the source of great frustration for everyone concerned. There are many situations where it is well understood that different "roles" are required to ask different questions, and this in itself is not necessarily a source of trouble. In business transactions, for instance, buyers and sellers are almost always asking different questions. That is inherent in their situation. I have never heard of a buyer, for example, who has asked himself, "How can I make sure this man makes the largest possible profit from this sale?" (The reason, incidentally, that used-car salesmen have such low credibility is that they are inclined to pretend that they are asking the same question as the potential car buyer, namely, "How can I get this car at the lowest possible price?" Since the buyer knows that the dealer cannot possibly be interested in this question, he is rightfully suspicious.) But in situations where it is assumed that different people will be asking roughly the same question—and they are not—we are faced with problems that are sometimes hard to discern. I have recently heard of a situation where a family vacation was marred because, without their knowing it, wife and husband were seeking answers to two quite different questions. The wife was asking, "How can we have a good time?" The husband was asking, "How can we get through this without spending too much money?" Two administrators who were trying to avoid bankruptcy provide another example: The first was asking, "How can we cut our staff?" The second, "How can we increase our income?" Naturally, their solutions moved in different directions. Finally, a pregnant woman and her obstetrician: The woman is asking, "How can I have my baby safely and with no unnecessary pain?" The doctor is asking, "How can this baby get born in time for me to have a full two-week vacation?"

I do not say that different questions are always incompatible in such situations. But they do have considerable potential for confusion if we are ignorant of their existence.

By-passing

In observing the ways in which people cope with each other's talk, I have noticed an extraordinary thing. You may wish to verify this for yourself if what I say sounds too facile or convenient. It is this: When one person makes an assertion to another (e.g., "*Jaws* is a terrible movie," "The unions have too much power," "The courts are coddling criminals," "Your friend is rather overbearing"), the hearer is inclined to respond in one of two ways —by agreeing or disagreeing. I am not implying that the response is literally "I agree" or "I disagree." But rather that it will usually take the form of a complementary or contradictory judgment to the one originally offered (e.g., "If you think *Jaws* was bad, you should see *Rollerball*" or "The unions don't have near as much power as they should").

There is, of course, at least a third way to respond to such assertions, and that is by asking, "What do you mean?" I have found that this alternative is infrequently used, and since it opens such an intelligent and appealing path to serious conversation, naturally I have wondered why.

There would appear to be two reasons—both understandable but also quite dangerous, unless under careful control. The first is that our assertions are not on all occasions invitations to begin serious talk. They are sometimes a form of terminal punctuation—the end rather than the beginning of conversation. S. I. Hayakawa has called such remarks "snarl" or "purr" sentences. Their function is merely to express an emphatic feeling or, possibly, to determine if the listener is of the same "tribe" as you. An astute listener will usually know when such assertions are serving that function and may wish to use the moment to get his own licks in, on the one hand, or to assure the speaker that their political or social or aesthetic sensibilities are roughly the same, on the other. In such circumstances, the question, "What do you mean?" is neither wanted nor necessary. A problem arises, however, when we become so habituated to agreeing or disagreeing that we forget how to respond in any other way. Then, in situations where clarification and precision are needed, we find ourselves purring or snarling our way through. Cases in point are not difficult to find. Everywhere we see fathers and sons, husbands and wives, employers and employees needing to understand what the other is saying but neglecting the means by which they can. "What do you mean?," when asked in a spirit of authentic inquiry, provides the road to such understanding. I do not say, by the way, that it assures *agreement*, but that it may generate a measure of light on the subject.

The second reason why "What do you mean?" is not employed as often as you might expect is more interesting (at least to me). The reason is suggested by the name which Irving Lee (I believe) gave to it: by-passing. By-passing is a process in which the following occurs: A says something to B. B assumes that A means what B would have meant if B had said those words in that situation to A. Therefore, there seems to be no necessity to inquire of A, "What do you mean?" B can go straight to the question, "Do I agree or disagree?" But, of course, this sort of assumption can be disastrous, as for example, when A has said something like "I love you." Now, "I love you" is a very important sentence and is probably spoken a thousand times every day in California alone. Of this sentence, we can be sure of very little except that its meaning depends wholly on the life-experience of the particular person using it. Thus, to assume that someone means by "I love you" what *you* would mean if you had said it to him or her is one of the more important pieces of stupidity around.

What do I suggest? Surely not to ask, "Exactly what do you mean by that?" when it's "I-love-you" time in some exotic and erotic setting. But since the consequences of such a sentence are fairly significant, it is not too much to suggest that at some point B will need to reflect on what A's meanings might be (as distinct from what B's meanings are). The search for what a person means by "I love you" will take you, of course, beyond words. It requires that you make observations of how a person behaves, not of what he or she says, since everyone says more or less the same things. But lovers are notoriously inept at making such observations. They frequently cannot see, through the haze of a few "I love you's," that the other is acting strangely or selfishly or even contemptibly. I suppose such observations are best made by relatives and friends, though their insights are rarely appreciated. It sometimes takes years before you realize that what someone meant by "I love you" or "I give you my word" or "I believe in total freedom" was not quite what you would have meant had you said those words.

But in a sense, by-passing is a "natural" form of stupidity. It occurs, I believe, because all communication depends, to some extent, on projection. In order to make any sense at all of what people are saying, we must assume that they are using words roughly in the same way we do. We put other people in our own skins, so to speak, and, therefore, to some extent, all our conversations are dialogues with ourselves, creations of our own imagination. We are apt to become aware of our projections only when someone's behavior is starkly different from what his words have led us to expect. A man who says, "I love you, darling," and then gives you a crack across the face and a kick in the shins is teaching you that talking to yourself has its limitations.

By-passing also occurs because of another "natural" form of stupidity. Since communication depends on an assumption of shared, predictable meanings, we are easily led to the belief that words, themselves, *have* meanings, and fixed ones, at that. But if there is anything certain in the whole field of human talk, it is that *words* do not have meanings. *People* do. And because people are different and perceive their purposes in different ways, the meanings they assign to words are not only *not* fixed but have wide variability. For this reason, when one is trying to clarify a communication problem, there is no more stupid question than, "What does this *word* mean?" What you need to know is what a particular *person* means (by that word in that situation). In 1896, for example, the nine men on the U.S. Supreme Court said that separate but equal facilities for blacks and whites are constitutional. In 1954, a different nine men said, in effect, that *separate* and *equal* are opposites; to quote Earl Warren, "Separate but equal is inherently unequal." It is rather pointless to ask, of course, what do *separate* and *equal* "really" mean? In the first place, who would know? *The New York Times?* Your ninth-grade English teacher? Webster's *Third?* The best they could do is to tell you how a word has tended to be used. But they cannot tell you how it will be used or, even more important, how it was used in some particular situation.

In the second place, what we require knowledge of is not the word but the *word-user*, and the circumstances and reasoning which generated the meaning he gave to it.

And so we have here a sort of paradox. On the one hand, we must naturally assume that others are using words to mean what we would, and that such meanings have some stability. But on the other hand, we must remember that this is only an assumption, that at any given moment a coin of the realm may not be worth quite what we imagined. And, naturally, our purposes will be short-changed.

Self-reflexiveness

(It is seven in the morning. The husband comes into the kitchen. He sits down and says, "Good morning." His wife says the same. Then, she places some bacon and eggs before him. He starts to eat.)

Husband: The bacon is a little crisp this morning.

Wife: What?

Husband: The bacon, it's way too crisp.

Wife: I always make it that way.

Husband: Not this way. It's too crisp. Almost burnt.

Wife: Well, why don't you make it yourself. Then, you can have it the way you want.

Husband: Really? Why don't *you* go to work. Then, you can have the *money* you want.

Wife: You don't call what I do work? If you paid me for what I do, you'd know it was work.

Husband: Pay you? For what? What the hell do you do?

Wife: More than you. I don't have time for two-hour lunches.

Husband: And I don't have time to watch "The Gathering Dust" all day.

Let's leave them for a moment, take a fast trot around the block, and come back two minutes later:

Husband: And, further, I don't want your mother coming here every other day.
Wife: My mother? What about your brother?

Let's leave them altogether now, but not what they have been doing. For this kind of talking is a perfect illustration of the "self-reflexive" nature of language, which is, and always will be, a source of considerable volumes of stupid talk. What self-reflexiveness means, as described in detail by Alfred Korzybski, is that using language is something like being in a mirrored room. No matter where you look, you will see yourself looking at a mirror. But you will also see yourself looking at a mirror which shows you looking at a mirror. And you will also see yourself looking at a mirror which shows you looking at a mirror which shows you looking at a mirror. And so on. The mirrors encase you, so to speak, in a "closed system," within which you get only reflections of reflections.

Language can be thought of as a reflection of reality. We try to say things that correspond to the processes and things outside of our skins. For example, "this bacon is too crisp." But once we say something about "reality," our listeners begin to be encased in the "mirror effect." Listeners must now respond not only to the "reality" our remarks referred to, but to our *remarks*, as well. They may not like, for example, our tone or point of view or form of address.

And so, they say something which refers in part to "reality" (e.g., the condition of the bacon) and in part to our language about "reality" (e.g., our tone). Now, it is our turn. We say something about what they said about what we said. They go. They say something about what we said about what they said about what we said. Before long, the "reality," two slices of overcooked (?) bacon, has been pushed out of the picture altogether, and our comments are exclusively motivated by the nature of comments, not by the nature of "reality."

There are several names that have been given to this process, one of which, coming from psychology, is "dyadic spiral." This name has the advantage of being a vivid metaphor which helps us to see how two people in conversation (a dyad) can get trapped in an ever-inwardly turning pattern from which it is very difficult to break free. But I prefer a term like "semantic self-reflexiveness," because it keeps our attention on the role that language itself plays in generating the problem.

One may argue, of course, that in the small scene I have constructed, there is no "problem"; that both husband and wife are simply ventilating some feelings that have been on their minds for quite a while; and that they will be better off for doing so. You may have gathered by now that I am not a strong believer in the "ventilation" theory of human communication, but even if I were, I would still insist that a "problem" of some significance has arisen in my domestic scene. In the first place, it is quite possible that the feelings being expressed in a situation of this sort are not especially "authentic" or deeply felt. They may originate solely from a desire to protect oneself from an attack. For all we know, the husband may admire his mother-in-law and not object in the least to her being a frequent houseguest. His wife may know perfectly well that her husband works quite hard and may harbor no resentment about his two-hour business lunches. But caught in the act of a talking process in which language is feeding on itself, people will sometimes reach out for hurtful things to say in order to maintain their position in the spiral. Therefore, if this be the case, both husband and wife are being led into saying things that they do not actually feel, and will not be better off for saying.

But even if their remarks do express genuinely felt antagonisms, it is important to say that the time, place, and form of such remarks are out of control. Aristotle spoke wisely on this point. "Anybody can become angry," he said, "that is easy, but to be angry with the right person, and to the right degree, and at the right time, and for the right purpose, and in the right way—that is not within everybody's power and is not easy." In short, the situation is doing all the talking here, and to the extent that the talkers cannot stop what is happening or redirect it, they are engaging in stupid talk, which they are almost certain to regret at some later date. It is almost always a "problem" when a semantic process has got going and you do not know how it started, and, especially, how to stop it.

Of course, if you are caught in a dyadic spiral, there is always the possibility that one of you will have the necessary knowledge and control to stop it when it is getting out of hand. For example, in my kitchen drama, there are several points at which the process could have been aborted. For instance:

> *Husband*: The bacon is a little crisp this morning.
> *Wife*: What?
> *Husband*: The bacon, it's way too crisp.
> *Wife*: I always make it that way.

(We have now approached the danger point. The bacon is about to disappear from the conversation. And even though it's seven in the morning, the following line is probably not too unrealistic.)

> *Husband*: Really? I must be getting old or something. I never noticed.
> *Wife*: Well, if you really don't like it that way, let me make another couple of slices.

Quite possibly, no one should say *anything* at seven in the morning. But if conversation is to take place, I see no reason why my last exchange is any more implausible than the first. Moreover, even if the conversation has gotten as far as, "And further, I don't want your mother coming here every other day," it is still quite possible to stop the torment with something like, "What on earth are we talking about? Look, if the bacon is too crisp, I'll make a couple of more pieces." This would take some courage to say, especially if one is not "in the mood." But if you remember that the "mood" is created in the first place by a semantic process of which you were not aware, it becomes easier to do it.

But the problem is compounded if a dyadic spiral is being conducted not by two people (one of whom may have the ability to stop it) but by one person—with himself. It is well known that most of the talking we do is with and to ourselves, and we are certainly not immune from driv-

ing ourselves stupid or crazy through the process of semantic self-reflexiveness. I am slightly embarrassed to repeat it because it is so old, but there is a joke which goes
right to the heart of this matter. It is about a man whose
tire goes flat on a dark and lonely country road. When
he discovers that he doesn't have a jack, he recalls seeing
a farm house about a mile back. And so he starts to walk
there in the hopes of borrowing one. While he is walking,
he talks to himself about his situation: "Wow, I'm really
stranded here. The guy will probably want a few dollars
to lend me his jack. Why should he do it for nothing?
Everyone wants to make a few bucks. A *few* bucks? If I
don't get the jack, I'll never get out of here. He'll realize
that, and probably want fifteen dollars, maybe twenty-
five dollars. Twenty-five dollars? This guy's really got me
by the old cashews. He'll ask fifty dollars, for sure—maybe
a hundred."

Well, he goes on in this way until he reaches the farm
house. He knocks at the door. An elderly farmer answers
and with a cheerful smile asks, "Is there something I can
do for you, young man?" "Do for me? Do for me?" says
the man, "I'll tell you what you can do, you can take your
goddamn jack and shove it!" And off he goes.

This joke, by the way, demonstrates two points at the
same time. The first is how self-reflexiveness works—how
we say things and then respond to what we said, and then,
to what we said about what we said about what we said,
etc. When the process is not under control, we can move
very far from the reality which started us talking in the
first place. The second point is a demonstration of what
Robert Merton has called "a self-fulfilling prophecy." A
self-fulfilling prophecy is a frequent consequence of self-

reflexiveness, taking the form of our making a prediction which comes true *because we have made the prediction*. If, as in this case, you predict that you will not be lent a jack in a spirit of gracious cooperation, you prepare yourself for the confrontation in such a way that you *guarantee* the jack will not be lent in a spirit of gracious cooperation. Your prediction is transformed into a fact, which then becomes the reality.

The self-fulfilling prophecy is at the core of what is usually meant by *stereotyping*, or *prejudice*. I happen to think, incidentally, that these words have had an undeservedly bad press; they have generally been discussed in a one-sided (entirely unfavorable) way. Stereotyping and prejudging are perfectly sensible—indeed, necessary— methods of predicting what is in store for us. When we go into a situation, we naturally prepare for it by categorizing, generalizing, and prophesying. To tell people to avoid doing this is to tell them to be stupid. When you go to see a dean, a doctor, or a deacon, you arrive with expectations. The more experience you have had with such people, the more detailed and comprehensive are your expectations. That is what we mean by knowledge and experience. The problem with stereotyping and prejudging is to avoid using them as self-fulfilling prophecies. If your expectations are too firmly fixed, you may not be able to see *anything* but your expectations. Moreover, you may well behave in such a way as to *insure* that your expectations will be fulfilled. Thus, you deprive yourself of the ability to see new and unexpected facts. Instead of enlarging your experience and knowledge, you contract them.

Suppose, for example, I am applying for a job. I will, naturally, collect all the information I can get about the situation, including the opinions of others, in order to predict what I will be asked, how I will be asked it, and what I will be told. This involves prejudgment and stereotyping. If I know that my prospective employer is roughly my own age and comes from the same background, I will plan certain strategies that would seem inappropriate if I knew him to be twice my age and from a completely different social class. So far, so good. The problem starts when I have come across an individual who, though he is my age and even from my neighborhood, acts as if he were much older and came from Sioux Falls. Of course, there is nothing whatever wrong with this. He is what he is. But I have already constructed a different picture of him in my imagination, and the question is, Will I maintain my picture, or will I make a new one to fit the facts? The great problem with most stereotypes and "prejudice" is not that there is no truth in them, but that there is just enough so that we may not see what is false. The dark side of prejudging and stereotyping is that they encourage us to hold on to old pictures, and, therefore, to act as if they were up-to-date. This is the "mirror effect" I referred to before. It is one thing—and quite inevitable—to see events through the window of our assumptions and expectations. It is quite another when the "window" is a mirror which only sends back those images we have projected onto it.

Thus, self-reflexiveness, stereotyping, prejudging, and even self-fulfilling prophecies are semantic processes by which we try to order and control our world. They form an essential part of what Adelbert Ames called "our assumptive world." We talk to ourselves about how we talk, because this is our way of evaluating what we have said about reality. We classify events, people, and things because this is our way of finding patterns and reducing the world to manageable dimensions. We generate expectations, because this is our way of preparing ourselves for what will happen to us. But our world becomes disorganized, unpredictable, and mystifying when we are not aware of exactly what we are doing and how we are doing it. To be unaware, for example, that one's anger can be generated more by one's own talk about an event than by the event itself means that the talk, not the talker, is the master. To assign more reality to a category of things than to a thing itself is to risk missing the variety and richness of experience. And to act as if one's predictions were established facts is to force onself into a mold which may have no applicability to the situation one is actually in.

Propaganda

Of all the words we use to talk about talk, *propaganda* is perhaps the most mischievous. The essential problems its use poses, and never resolves, are reflected in the following definition, given by no less a personage than the late Aldous Huxley:

> There are two kinds of propaganda—rational propaganda in favor of action that is consonant with the enlightened self-interest of those who make it and those to whom it is addressed, and nonrational propaganda that is not consonant with anybody's enlightened self-interest, but is dictated by, and appeals to, passion.

This definition is, of course, filled with confusion and even nonsense, both of which are uncharacteristic of Huxley and only go to show how *propaganda* can bring the best of us down.

To begin with, Huxley makes a distinction between "good" and "bad" propaganda on the basis of the cause

being espoused. If what we are told is good for everybody, then propaganda is "rational." If it is bad for everybody, it is nonrational. But how are we to know what is
good and what is bad for everybody? In most instances,
this is far from self-evident, and not even an Aldous Huxley can say for sure what is enlightened and what is not.
Moreover, the information we might need to decide the
issue is often not available to us. Suppose, for example, a
television commercial tells us that a certain drug will help
to relieve nagging backaches. That would appear to be in
everybody's self-interest, thus, rational propaganda. But
let us also suppose it is later discovered that in addition to
relieving nagging backaches, the drug also relieves you of
a healthy liver. Was the commercial "good" propaganda
at the time you heard it or was it "bad"? Perhaps it was
"good" when you heard it but *became* "bad" when you
learned of the drug's side-effects. But since it was never in
anybody's self-interest to use the drug, then wasn't the
commercial "bad" propaganda to begin with?

And now let us suppose that in combination with another substance, the drug is rendered harmless to your
liver. Will a commercial for the drug (with Secret Formula X-gy added) now be "good" propaganda? Then
suppose. . . . Well, you can begin to see the problems here.

But they are simple ones compared to those raised by a
television commercial which tells us to vote for a political
candidate. How would we know *before* the candidate is
elected if it is in everybody's self-interest to vote for him?
Indeed, how would we know a year after his election if it
has been in everybody's self-interest? People continually
disagree over such matters, and we would be left with a
definition of propaganda that says: What I think has been

good for me is "rational." What you think has been good for you is "nonrational." But Huxley does give us a hint, although a misleading one, of how we may resolve the problem. He says that nonrational propaganda "appeals to passion." He says nothing about the type of appeal made by rational propaganda, but we may assume he believes it appeals to the "intellect." Here Huxley has, of course, moved to another ground, and is offering a definition based on the type of appeal, not the goodness or badness of the cause. But as he has it here, this shift only results in more confusion. What do we say of "propaganda" that appeals to our passions but in an enlightened cause? And what of propaganda that appeals to our intellect but for a cause that is not consonant with everybody's enlightened self-interest?

There are two possible ways out of this dilemma, as far as I can see. The first is to stop using the word "propaganda" altogether. Huxley himself seems to suggest this in another part of the book, from which I earlier quoted. He says:

> In regard to propaganda the early advocates of universal literacy and a free press envisaged only two possibilities: the propaganda might be true, or it might be false. They did not foresee what in fact has happened ... the development of a vast mass communications industry, concerned in the main neither with the true nor the false, but with the unreal, the more or less totally irrelevant.

I infer from this passage that Huxley does not quite know how to classify "totally irrelevant" messages except to say that they are nonrational because they distract peo-

ple from seeing the "truth." Of course, they also distract
people from seeing "falsehoods," and perhaps on that
account, Huxley might think, as I do, that the word
"propaganda" causes more misunderstanding than it resolves.

But if the word is to remain with us, then I suggest we
pick up on one of Huxley's ideas and use "propaganda" to
refer not to the goodness or badness of causes but exclusively to a use of language designed to evoke a particular
kind of response. We might say, for example, that propaganda is language that invites us to respond emotionally,
emphatically, more or less immediately, and in an either-
or manner. It is distinct from language which stimulates
curiosity, reveals its assumptions, causes us to ask questions, invites us to seek further information and to search
for error. From this perspective, we eliminate the need to
distinguish between good and bad propaganda (except in
the sense that "good" propaganda works and "bad"
doesn't). We eliminate the need to focus on causes and
actions and the precarious issue of which ones are in
whose enlightened self-interest. And we eliminate the
need, which thankfully Huxley does not bring up but
which others have, to distinguish between language that
persuades and language that doesn't. Since all language
is purposive (even, I am told, the language of paranoid
schizophrenics: "Well, I'll be damned. Dead men *do*
bleed!"), we can assume that talking is always intended as
some form of persuasion. Thus, the distinction between
persuasion and other types of talking does not seem to be
very useful. But the distinction between language that
says "Believe this" and language that says, "Consider this"

is, in my opinion, certainly worth making, and especially because the techniques of saying "Believe this" are so various and sophisticated. Here, for example, are two pieces of propaganda, according to the way in which I have defined the word. The first is of a fairly obvious species, and I think three short paragraphs of it will be about all you can take. It was published in *The Indianapolis Star* in 1968, about the time the Vietnam War was heating up, and was called "A Letter From a War Veteran":

> It was too bad I had to die in another country. The United States is so wonderful, but at least I died for a reason, and a good one.
>
> I may not understand this war, or like it, or want to fight it, but nevertheless I had to do it, and I did.
>
> I died for the people of the United States. I died really for you; you were my one real happiness. I died also for your mom and dad so that they could go on working. . . . For your brothers so that they could play sports in freedom without Communist rule. . . .

It goes on like this for several paragraphs, in the course of which God comes into the picture, along with Dad's retirement, vacations, and several other sure-fire winners. There is, in my opinion, not much to say of interest about this piece of propaganda because it is so obviously constructed to evoke Indianapolis passions in favor of the war. This is not to say that there were no arguments for waging the war, only that no arguments are presented here in any form, and there is no pretense that there are. The rhetorical devices are, so to speak, all up front, and I confess to a certain admiration for the boldness of their sentimentality. Even the admen on Madison Avenue would be ashamed to try to pull this off, and I can't help thinking that there must be something very curious going on in Indiana if this could be done as late as 1968.

But the next species of propaganda is another matter. In fact, perhaps in a special way, it illuminates the difference between Indiana stupid talk and New York stupid talk. This one was widely circulated among intellectuals in New York City when it was the fashion to elevate revolutionaries to sainthood.

The propaganda was intended to give us some background information on George Jackson, who was for a time a charismatic leader in the movement for black liberation. We are informed that Jackson was a choirboy, that his father was a post office employee, and that Jackson subscribed to conventional values when he was young. We are also told that the circumstances of Jackson's first serious crime were these: One night a friend whom Jackson had invited for a ride in his car ordered him to stop at a gas station. The friend went inside and stole seventy dollars; then he told Jackson to drive away. Although Jackson was convicted for robbery, we are led to believe that he was entirely innocent. The following paragraph telling of Jackson's early life was included in the piece as part of our background information:

When Jackson was 15, still too young to drive legally, he had a slight accident in his father's car, knocking a few bricks out of the outside wall of a small grocery store near his home. His father paid the damages, the store owner refrained from pressing charges, but he was still sent to reform school for driving without a license.

Three years later, shortly after his release from reform
school, he made a down payment on a motorbike, which
turned out to have been stolen. His mother had the receipt and produced it for the police, but Jackson was
sent back to reform school, this time for theft.

I believe that this paragraph is one of the great propagandistic passages of all time, and is deserving of being
included in the *Joseph Goebbels Casebook of Famous
Boondoggles*. Let us do a small explication of it:

When Jackson was 15, still too young to drive legally. . . .

Well, now, what does this imply? That Jackson was a
competent driver, but that the laws governing these matters are unreasonable? Why not, "still too young to drive"?
Who or what is in need of correction here, Jackson or the
Motor Vehicle Bureau?

. . . he had a slight accident in his father's car, knocking
a few bricks out of the outside wall of a small grocery
store near his home . . .

The diminutives are almost oppressive: a *slight* accident, a *few* bricks, a *small* grocery store. One almost
expects to read that someone's *trivial* leg was *barely* frac-
tured. And what is a slight accident, anyway? Dislodging
even a few bricks from an *outside* wall (It wasn't, for
God's sake, an *inside* wall!) doesn't sound awfully slight
to me. And why are we told it was "near his home"? Are
we being led to believe that he had only driven around
the block?

Best of all is the phrase "in his father's car." Does this imply that George really had nothing to do with the accident, that it happened *to* him while he was innocently sitting in his father's car? Why not, "He had a slight accident when he stole his father's car"? Or did George's father approve of his taking the car?

> His father paid the damages. The store owner refrained from pressing charges, but he was still sent to reform school for driving without a license.

The "still" is a wonderful piece of propaganda here. It leads us to believe that everything had been settled to everyone's satisfaction, but that the police and the courts were simply being vindictive. After all, it was a *small* crime, and George *was* a choirboy. Why the big deal?

> Three years later, shortly after his release from reform school, he made a down payment on a motorbike, which turned out to have been stolen.

First of all, I'd like to know how "shortly" after his release. It sounds as if George was in reform school for almost three years. Is this true? And why is the information being kept from me?

Second, the word "down payment" is simply marvelous. It conjures an image of a responsible businessman engaged in a wholly legitimate transaction. But George obviously didn't buy the motorbike at Macy's. He must have bought it from someone on the streets who was giving him a "real bargain." But, the "turned out to be stolen" suggests that choirboy George never suspected, not even for a moment, that anyone could traffic in stolen property. Where did George grow up, in Beverly Hills?

> His mother had the receipt and produced it for the police, but Jackson was sent back to reform school, this time for theft.

The implication here is that the evidence George's mother produced should have been enough for any reasonable policeman. But apparently it wasn't. What was the evidence against George? Was he convicted of theft without a trial? What did the police have to say at the trial? We are told nothing, left with the impression that George was possibly framed and certainly the victim of a system that was out to get him.

Let me stress, in case you have gotten the wrong impression, that I do not know much about the late George Jackson, and most of what I do know evokes my admiration. What I am talking about is a method of propagandizing which attempts to conceal itself as information. The response that is asked for here is, "Believe this. You are being given all the information you need to know." But I can sooner believe that a soldier would go to war for Mom's apple pie than that a friend of George invited him for a ride, "ordered" him to stop at a gas station, held up the place, and told him to drive away, while all the time George thought his friend was only going to the bathroom. I would guess that you couldn't get away with that kind of stuff in Indianapolis. . . . In New York, it's easy.

Each end of the political spectrum has, I suppose, its own favorite style of propaganda. The Right tends to prefer gross, straightforward sentimentality. The Left, a sort of surface intellectualizing. But it is very important, it seems to me, to note that the response required of us, in each instance, is a passionate, uncritical acceptance of a point of view.

I am not implying, by the way, that there is no legitimate function for propaganda. There are several semantic environments—advertising, for example—where it is quite reasonable for one person to ask another to believe what he is saying. In fact, much of our literature—especially, popular literature—amounts to a direct appeal to our emotions. To the extent that such appeals are cathartic or entertaining or, in some sense, a stimulus to self-discovery, they are invaluable. In other words, propaganda is not, by itself, a problem, if it comes dressed in its natural clothing. But when it presents itself as something else, regardless of the cause it represents, it is a form of stupid talk that can be, and has been, extremely dangerous. It is dangerous for two reasons. First, propaganda demands a way of responding which can become habitual. If we allow ourselves, too easily, to summon the emotions that our own causes require, we may be unable to hold them back when confronted with someone else's causes. And second, propaganda has a tendency to work best on groups rather than individuals. It has the effect of turning groups into crowds, which is what Huxley calls "herd poisoning." As he describes it, herd poisoning is "an active, extraverted drug. The crowd-intoxicated individual escapes from responsibility, intelligence, and morality into a kind of frantic, animal mindlessness."

Here, Huxley is talking about what happens when an individual has joined with other individuals in a semantic environment where propaganda, unchecked, is doing its work. Stupid talk is transformed into an orgy of crazy talk, the consequences of which can be found in graves stretching from Siberia to Mississippi to Weimar to Peking. (This last sentence is, of course, propaganda, pure and simple, but I like it, anyway.)

Eichmannism

Eichmannism is a form of talk which takes its name from the notoriously efficient bureaucrat, Adolf Eichmann, who was instrumental in arranging for the murder of over one million people. Unlike Paul Blobel and other certifiable Nazi psychotics, Eichmann did not appear to be motivated by excessive devotion to his *Führer*. Nor did he believe that those who were being sent to their deaths were suffering less than those who were sending them. And when he stood in the dock in Jerusalem, he actually said, with apparent sincerity, that some of his best friends were Jews.

Eichmann was, by most accounts, a fairly "reasonable" man, and at his trial, he maintained that it was unfair and gratuitously vindictive to punish him since he was merely doing his job. It was not *his* idea to send people to the gas chamber, and, in fact, it is fairly clear that he was not the sort of man who naturally thinks of such things. Eichmann merely had extraordinary administrative abilities that made him an excellent choice to solve certain complicated logistical problems; for example, how to get thousands of people onto trains so that they could be moved to a place of extermination. Eichmann himself never visited that place, because he felt sure it would make him sick, as indeed it probably would have.

The point about Eichmannism is that we all have the potential for it in varying degrees. There is not one of us, I imagine, who has not participated in some process whose goal we did not approve of or whose goal we carefully avoided seeking to know. Yet, we participated because our job required it or someone depended on us. Of course, I do not say that all of us could do what Eichmann did, or anything resembling it. Only that, as Professor Milgram demonstrated, we are capable of doing acts of stupidity or cruelty without really meaning to. Milgram explains this by saying that "relationship overwhelms content," by which he means that maintaining our role and status in a situation is apt to be more important to us than the overall purpose of the situation itself. I have no doubt that this explanation is sound, but I should like to broaden it somewhat to include the point of view of the French sociologist Jacques Ellul. To Ellul, a person's relationship to others in a semantic environment is only one aspect of a larger complex of forces, all of which he calls *la technique*. Technique includes all of the methods, media, and materials through which human behavior is organized and controlled. In this sense, not only are an account book, a conveyer belt, and a television set techniques, but so is a restaurant. Its tables, its silverware, its decor, its menus, its waiters—these are all part of a complex ensemble for making people behave in certain ways.

Parliamentary procedure is a technique for controlling how people will talk and what they may say. So is a courtroom, a classroom, a barroom, and a living room. Technique, in Ellul's sense, is obviously quite similar to what I have been calling a semantic environment. It is the totality of organizing principles which govern a situation.

Now, it frequently happens, as Ellul has abundantly documented, that people become so preoccupied with technique that their power—indeed, even will—to think about purpose is greatly diminished. This is especially the case where technique is extremely complex and requires great concentration to learn and to perform adequately. For example, if you have never before been in a restaurant or a courtroom or a classroom, you will, upon entering one, become so engaged in coping with its rules, its language, and its design that you will barely have anything left over to think about *why* you are there in the first place. But even after you have become accustomed to such situations, the complexity of their techniques is likely to keep you sufficiently busy so that you cannot concentrate on purpose. A simple way of saying this is that the *how* of a situation tends to overwhelm the *why*. In fact, it is not unusual for the "how" to *become* the "why," as for example, in our space program, where technique is so complex and demanding and interesting that we end up thinking that the reason we are doing what we are doing is—well, to do what we are doing. I do not say that no one has offered other reasons as to why we go into outer space. But it is obvious that such reasons are thought up after the fact, by people who are essentially fascinated, perhaps even hypnotized, by the process.

One of the words commonly used to describe people in this condition of preoccupation is technocrat, and, up to a point, we are all technocrats, since without a competent interest in and control over the techniques of our environment, nothing could get done. Even a simple conversation between two people involves the use of technique—a practical knowledge of what the rules are. To use technique is no moral defect. Neither does it necessarily generate stupid talk or crazy talk. But what I am here calling Eichmannism is that degree of commitment to technique that makes it come before all other considerations, especially the meaning and consequences of the system within which one is operating. The devoted men who surrounded Richard Nixon were just doing their job, and a difficult one at that. Covering up crimes is hard enough to do without the added burden of deciding *whether* to do it. This obliviousness to responsibility for consequences is Eichmannism.

In America, where complex technique is apt to be highly valued, if not revered, Eichmannism is a fairly familiar kind of talk. And it is important to say that it is almost always polite, subdued, and sometimes even gracious, in a plastic sort of way. A friend of mine once received a letter from an administrator which began, "We are pleased to inform you that your scholarship for the [coming] academic year has been canceled." That *pleased to inform you* tells us a great deal: that the person who wrote it did not really understand what his letter was about or what its consequences might be. Perhaps he did not *want* to understand. The important thing was to get the letter done and go on to the next matter of business.

My most treasured Eichmannism, however, comes from

a schoolteacher who addressed the following letter to ninth-grade students just before the Christmas holidays. It is worth reading, I think, because it contains all the symptoms of the "problem" in an exquisitely compact form:

Dear Student:
May I take this opportunity to wish each and every one a very holy and merry holiday season. Kindly extend this greeting to the members of your household and those who will help you celebrate this festive time of year.

Writers remind us constantly that with the arrival of a new year, we must become cognizant of the fact that it is time to proclaim our New Year's resolutions. As a class, let us accept for the theme of the New Year the ever-powerful meaning of the need and desire for "Enthusiasm." Remember, my dear students, that "Enthusiasm" can and will achieve the unheard of and the miraculous. Place within your minds and the deep recesses of your hearts the need for enthusiasm. An unknown writer once said: "Carry enthusiasm in your attitude and manner; it spreads like a contagion; it begets and inspires effects you did not dream of."

To aid and guide you on your pathway to learning, the following assignments will help you to activate vehemently your newly acquired aim, "Enthusiasm."
1. A vocabulary test will be given the day that you return to school.
Period One: "Nouns and Verbs" and "Workaday Words"
Period Four: The words which were given to you on Monday, December 10
2. Oral book reports will be given the first week of

school. Prepare to answer the following questions about
the book you read.

1. Give the title, author, publisher, and date of pub-
lication.

2. What was the theme of the story?

3. What was the setting of the story? Discuss the importance of the setting in this particular story.

4. Do a character study of one major character. Be
sure to give specific information from the reading that
will back up any general statement you may make
about this character.

We must remember the reality of the fact that we are
beginning a program of study that will mold our future.
This presents to us responsibilities. I did not prepare this
epistle to harass you, but I sincerely wish to prepare you
for the demands of high school and college, with which
some of you will be confronted in the near future.

I once again extend to you and your family my season's greetings.

What this letter is about, of course, is a couple of tests
and assignments which the teacher is rather hard put to
justify. I would almost go so far as to say that what this
teacher's *classroom* is about is tests and assignments, the
purposes of which have long since been forgotten, if
they were ever known. To conceal their absence, even
from himself, the teacher surrounds the assignments with
fairly preposterous homilies and long-range projections of
how they will "activate vehemently your newly acquired
aim, 'Enthusiasm.'" This is a rather pathetic attempt to
raise to a level of glory a more or less trivial technique
of measurement. Is it conceivable that a ninth-grade student, anywhere in the world, would prepare for those post-

holiday assignments with the expectation that in doing so, he or she is assuming new and life-giving responsibilities? And yet, there is no irony in the language of this letter. This is serious business, and in that respect it is choice Eichmannism. Eichmannism is talk that tries to ennoble technique, to make it appear that the Kingdom of Heaven awaits those who follow the proper routine.

One may find such talk in many semantic environments throughout our culture. In sex manuals, for example, where it is generally implied that joy does not come from why sex is done but how. Or in guides to raising children, where you discover that your failure as a parent derives almost solely from ignorance of the proper technique. Even a book like this one runs the risk of creating the impression that crazy talk or stupid talk is merely a matter of one's using the wrong technique. That is why I have taken such pains to emphasize the purposes of talk. To talk about talk without respect to purpose is an example of Eichmannism.

And yet, Eichmannism has some curious variations. There is, for example, what I call Skinnerism, which, of course, takes its name from America's foremost behaviorist, B. F. Skinner. Skinnerism is, in one sense, the opposite of Eichmannism, but in another sense, they are the same. It is the opposite in that it appears to be goal- or purpose-oriented. It is a technique for producing specific changes in behavior. It asks of you, What sort of behavior do you feel is desirable? And then, it proceeds through "operant conditioning" to produce such behavior. But it is the same as Eichmannism in that its practitioners do not sufficiently appreciate the power of technique to influence purpose. They assume that it makes no difference how you arrive at some goal, as long as you get there. Reason, fear, and approval are only means to an end, and "positive reinforcement" is chosen because it is the most efficient. If fear were more so, it would be used instead. But that is the quintessential fallacy of Eichmannism: Eichmannism represents the triumph of technique. It may take the form of our downgrading ends in favor of means, or it may take the subtler form of downgrading the means by which we will achieve our ends. To say that "I do not want to think about why I am doing this, only about how I do it" is not very different from saying, "I do not want to think about how I am doing this, only about why." In both instances, technique reigns supreme. In the former because we have given it all our consideration. In the latter, because we have given it none.

Definition Tyranny

One of the more curious federal laws now in existence concerns what you may not say when being "frisked" or otherwise examined before boarding an airplane. You may not, of course, give false or misleading information about yourself. But beyond that, you are also expressly forbidden to "joke" about any of the procedures being used. This is the only semantic environment I know of where a joke is prohibited by law (although there are many situations in which it is prohibited by custom).

Why joking is illegal when you are being searched is not entirely clear to me, but that is only one of several mysteries surrounding this law. Does the law distinguish, for example, between good jokes and bad jokes? (Six months for a good one, two years for a bad one?) I don't know. But even more important, how would one know when something is a "joke" at all? Suppose, while being searched, I mention that my middle name is Milton (which it is) and that I come from Flushing (which I do).

I can tell you from experience that people of questionable intelligence sometimes find those names extremely funny, and it is not impossible that a few of them are airport employees. If that were the case, what would be my legal status? I have said something which has induced laughter in another. Have I, therefore, told a "joke"? Or look at it from the opposite view: Suppose that, upon being searched, I launch into a story about a funny thing that happened to me while boarding a plane in Chicago, concluding with the line, "And then the pilot said, 'That was no stewardess. That was my wife.' " Being of questionable intelligence myself, I think it is a hilarious story, but the guard does not. If he does not laugh, have I told a joke? Can a joke be a story that does *not* make people laugh?

It can, of course, if someone of authority says so. For the point is that in every situation, including this one, someone (or some group) has a decisive power of definition. In fact, to have power means to be able to define and to make it stick. As between the guard at the airport and me, he will have the power, not me, to define what a "joke" is. If his definition places me in jeopardy, I can, of course, argue my case at a trial, at which either a judge or a jury will then have the decisive authority to define whether or not my words qualified as a "joke." But it is also worth noting that even if I confine my joke-telling to dinner parties, I do not escape the authority of definition. For at parties, popular opinion will decide whether or not my jokes are good ones, or even jokes at all. If opinion runs against me, the penalty is that I am not invited to many parties.

There is, in short, no escaping the jurisdiction of definitions. Social order requires that there be established definitions (sometimes fixed and formal, sometimes fluid and informal), and though you may search from now to doomsday, you will find no system without official definitions (of some sort) and authoritative sources (of some sort) to enforce them.

Some people, however, are greatly tyrannized by definitions. They seem unable to put any distance between themselves and a system's way of defining things. I am not talking here about one's "accepting" a definition on pragmatic grounds. This may be necessary in order to function within a system. You may think, for example, that defining a corporation as a "person" is pretty silly stuff, but you will have to "accept" it if you are to understand and participate in America's corporate structure. What I am talking about is people who have so internalized a definition that they cannot even imagine an alternative way of seeing matters. They make *a* definition into *the* definition, and, as a consequence, sharply limit their ability to evaluate what is happening to them. After all, one ought to know what is happening even if one cannot always change it. Here, for example, is the beginning of a letter written by a college student who has, happily for him, refused to internalize the psychological legitimacy of a certain definition (although he "accepts," no doubt, its legality):

Dear Admissions Officer:
I am in receipt of your rejection of my application. As much as I would like to accommodate you, I find I cannot accept it. I have already received four rejections from other colleges, and this number is, in fact, over my limit. Therefore, I must reject your rejection, and as

much as this might inconvenience you, I expect to appear for classes on September 18 . . .

More than likely, this letter will not change the status of the student, but it reveals a certain liberated spirit to his way of thinking. He is a grown-up version of the little child in *The Emperor's New Clothes*. He will insist upon putting forward his own definition of the situation even if others will not see it that way, and even if it will not change things. He has, in fact, reversed the system's definition. It is not *his* application that is inadequate. It is the college's rejection slip.

It goes almost without saying, then, that I regard our capacity to maintain a certain psychological distance from conventional definitions to be a valuable asset in protecting ourselves against the onset of stupid or crazy talk. To have to speak someone else's words, to have all of our attitudes governed by someone else's definitions, can be a very dangerous situation. Therefore, you might find it useful in avoiding "definition tyranny" to consider the following questions the next time you are told that something is or is not a "joke," a "sin," a "failure," an "illness," or anything else.

Who or what is the source of the definition? What is the source of its-his-her authority? Political Power? Economic Power? Legal Power? Tradition Power? Public Opinion Power? Knowledge Power? (Here I might say that some people derive their authority from the fact that they know more than the rest of us. If you are a novice skier, for example, you will usually allow an experienced skier to define what are "safe" conditions. If you are not feeling well, you will probably permit a physician to define what "medication" is.) To what extent have you participated in granting this authority? To what extent do you regard the method by which it was granted to be "rational," "just," "moral," etc. What attitudes toward yourself and others are promoted by this definition? What are some of its important consequences? What assumptions about people underlie the definition? What alternative definitions are you aware of? Who are the people who have offered them? What are their motives? What purposes might they have in mind? To what extent can you play a role in changing the definition? Who will be helped by a different definition? Who will be hurt?

Finally, I should like to put before you a relevant observation made by Paul Watzlawick (et al.) in *The Pragmatics of Human Communication*: ". . . crazy communication (behavior) is not necessarily the manifestation of a 'sick' mind, but may be the only possible reaction to an absurd or untenable communications context." There are two ideas here worth thinking about, in my opinion. The first is that it sometimes happens that we find ourselves in an environment whose definitions are so utterly irrational that we can at no point grant their legitimacy without becoming "crazy." If, for example, we are part of a system which defines certain groups of people as subhuman (e.g., blacks, Jews), we cannot accept such a definition without, fairly soon, beginning to talk and act a little crazy. The second idea is that if we reject such a definition, and refuse to act on it, those to whom the definition seems reasonable will think *us* crazy. And so, it would appear that we lose either way. We are "crazy" when we accept irrational or evil definitions. And we are "crazy" when we do not (if everyone else does). It is a bad situation, but I am inclined to think that the second crazy has given our species some of its finest moments. The first has not, and, I think, never will.

Sloganeering

Maybe it is true (and maybe it isn't) that battles are won on the playing fields of schools. But certainly something is lost there. For on playing fields and in gymnasiums everywhere, people are encouraged to practice a peculiar variety of stupid talk which they later on bring to perfection at political rallies and other rituals of mass ecstasy. I am referring to what I call sloganeering, which in the wrong semantic environment can be transformed into an especially lethal form of crazy talk.

Sloganeering consists largely of ritualistic utterances that are intended to communicate solidarity. "On, Wisconsin!" would be a typical example. "Power to the people!" would be another. "Let's go, Mets!" would be one more. And, of course, "*Sieg heil!*"

It would be shallow to deny that such highly ritualistic sayings and/or chantings have some useful social functions and may even satisfy a deeply rooted aesthetic need. Children, for example, will frequently indulge in singing slogans at each other. And at religious ceremonies, there are many occasions when the congregation sings, chants, or speaks certain prayers whose power is amplified by collective recitation. And, of course, almost everyone loves a community sing. Apparently, there is something to this form of group talking that is part of what people call human nature. It is surely one of the principal ways by which we may suppress our individuality and align ourselves, wholeheartedly, with a community sentiment. One might even say that community consciousness is given its most direct expression through such group performances. If you add to this the aesthetic satisfaction most of us derive from simply saying meaningless sounds, like "Barney Google with the Goo Goo Googley Eyes," you can account for the universal practice of group chanting, cheering, and screaming.

I do not intend to say, therefore, that in all circumstances such verbal behavior is either stupid or crazy. If Columbia is on the verge of pulling off the upset of the century over Michigan State, provided it can move the ball three yards in four tries, almost any reasonable man will scream his lungs out in the hope that the gods which control such matters are also reasonable and will hear. Nonetheless, I do think it is worth remarking, briefly, on the dangers of such behavior. The distance between "Go, Go, Go, Lions" and "Off the Pigs" is not so great as some people suppose. A man who would say the former is at least a *candidate* for saying the latter. Unless he has matters firmly under control.

The first thing, then, that needs to be stressed is that sloganeering, by definition, is a repudiation of individual thought, another example of what Huxley calls "herd poisoning." Even when the slogan comes from the mouth of a single person, as when someone says (or used to say), "Right on!" we are hearing a group speak, not an individual. The purpose of such slogans is to signal that one is a member of a special class of people. This is accomplished by saying exactly what any other member of the group would say. Sometimes this can be very useful in helping you to know what sort of situation you are in. For example, if you should say "hello" to someone and get a reply such as "The Lord be with you" or "Power to the people, brother," you will know how to prepare yourself for the next few minutes. Of course, "hello" is, in itself, a highly ritualized remark—a slogan, if you will—but it does not commit you to any other classification than that of an English-speaking member of the human race. Moreover, "hello," "good morning," or any similar expression merely indicates a desire to engage in a civilized transaction. It does not imply that you adhere to any special religious, political, or social doctrine. That implication is, of course, characteristic of the type of sloganeering I am talking about. It is a form of group-think. It says, "This is what *we* believe," not, "This is what *I* believe." Or more precisely, it says, "This is what we *feel*," since most slogans cannot exactly be called beliefs. "All power to the people," for example, hardly qualifies as a human thought. Or if it does, its meaning (as anything but a group marker) is hopelessly muddled. Very few sloganeers who have used this expression could possibly want "the people" to have all that "power," since (I would guess) a majority of people in this country are opposed to the various causes which such a sloganeer usually favors. More likely, the sloganeer means "All power to *our* people, and to hell with the others." Which *is* a thought of sorts, and a delightfully candid one, at that. But it would not make an entirely satisfactory slogan. It lacks, for example, a singsong meter. In fact, if you change "All power to the people" to some obviously meaningless phrase such as "All putty to the pee pee," you can hear how delightful is its music. Thus, "All power to *our* people, and to hell with the others" would not do—on aesthetic grounds alone. But it also lacks the moral authority that a reputable slogan tries to project. An important characteristic of most slogans is that they will try to convey a high moral stance, as, for example, in "Free all political prisoners" or "Keep America beautiful" or "Make love, not war." The moral purity of these slogans is achieved mostly through their simplicity, the elimination of all contradiction and ambiguity. To introduce a note of discord or to suggest that there are those who would suffer at your hands would result in re-flection, not fervor. In short, the key to a good slogan is that it makes no distinctions other than the basic one be-tween good guys and bad guys. Slogans, after all, are in-tended to go beyond our reasoning and penetrate to places where our emotions are stored. What they hope to elicit is an instantaneous response, or what some seman-ticists call a *signal reaction*. A signal reaction is what hap-pens when words have lost their referential or symbolic aspect and instead assume the character of religious icons. A good Christian, for example, is not usually expected to inquire into what a crucifix stands for, or how it came to be used. In the presence of a crucifix, he is expected to react, to feel—for a crucifix is not exactly a thought, but a catalyst for the release of emotions. In saying this, I am not ridiculing the use of crucifixes or other religious icons. Within the semantic environment of religion (as well as, for example, the theater), signal reactions are entirely necessary and useful. But when the signal reaction becomes the standard method of response in semantic environments where inquiry and complex thought are required, we are on very dangerous ground. "Deutschland über Alles" is not exactly human language. It is, like the American flag, a command to feel, and we are not expected to ask why, or what does it mean, or where does it come from? "Better dead than red," "Freedom now," "Liberty, equality, and fraternity"—these are icons whose effect is to reduce the range and power of human insight. They imply that certain questions have been settled (or that there was no question to begin with) and that all that is required is collective commitment and passion.

As I suggested earlier, the roots of sloganeering doubtless go very deep, and there are few semantic environments in which some form of mindless recitation is not encouraged. Sloganeering, is, in fact, practiced in seemingly inexhaustible variety, in pledges, oaths, banners, bumper stickers, college cheers, mantras—wherever it appears desirable to ease the burden of individual responsibility for thinking a matter through.

As a general rule, whenever you find yourself applauding, cheering, or chanting in public places, you may suspect that your intelligence has been by-passed, and that someone has raised before your eyes a verbal crucifix. Knowing this, you may wish to applaud, cheer, or chant, anyway, on the grounds that it is good for you to "let go." Or perhaps you will feel the need to submerge yourself in a collectivized mood. But unless there is some part of you that knows exactly what is happening and which has retained the option to withdraw, you are participating in a fairly dangerous exhibition of stupid talk.

Arguments

Let me say at once that, so far as I can tell, there are nearly as many reasons why people have arguments as there are people who have them. Included among these reasons is that having arguments provides some people with a "personality," through which they may become forces to be reckoned with. If you have little else to recommend your notice by other people, you can certainly command their attention by hollering, making accusations, and coming to unshakable conclusions.

Then, too, an argument is a resourceful way of giving expression to certain antagonisms that a situation may prohibit from being openly revealed. If, for example, you deeply resent another person because he has more money or social status than you, you may find it profitable (and even agreeable) to argue with him about the state of the union or some other matter on which you and he disagree. If you can "win," life is bound to be a bit sweeter. If you lose, well, there's always another argument to be had.

There are also people (all of us) who would like to understand some issue but who do not have the time, patience, or background to go into it too deeply. Therefore, when it comes up, rather than concede our weakness, it is not too difficult to create the impression that our knowledge equals our interest by starting an argument. Sometimes, of course, we just don't want to be left out of a conversation, and starting an argument seems as good a way as any of getting into the thick of things.

To these reasons, and many others of a similar nature, I will not address myself. A thorough and useful analysis of the psychological motives for arguments is well beyond my knowledge (although I am prepared to argue with certain people that it is not). Instead, I am concerned here with a particular kind of argument, one with the following characteristics: It gets started when you do not really want it to; it has deprived you of learning something you would really like to know about; and it has occurred not because of some deep and hidden feelings, but because of a lack of awareness of how language works. In short, I am saying that people sometimes start shouting at each other, take unrelenting "positions," make dogmatic assertions, cite mythical facts, and, in general, try to "win" their conversations not because they "need" to (in a deep psychological sense), but rather because they have been victimized by some semantic process which they cannot control. The kind of argument I am talking about is one that starts off as an "intelligent discussion" but somewhere along the way is transformed into an exchange of stupid talk, which everyone later on regrets. My inquiries have led me to think that there are at least seven important reasons why such situations develop.

The first three I have already discussed in varying detail. For example, the first is the problem posed by semantic self-reflexiveness. I will not say much more about this except to repeat that ignorance of when it is happening may take us so far from a subject that after four or five minutes we can no longer locate it. And having lost the subject, we have nothing left to talk about except the manner in which we are talking. A second reason, also discussed, is by-passing. Of this, I will say, again, that the tendency to respond to assertions as if their meanings were self-evident is a frequent cause of the erosion of discussion and inquiry. Even in cases where technical words are largely being employed, it can be a mistake to assume that others mean what you mean by them. And a good way to keep argument at a distance is to raise to a level of consciousness how everyone is using certain key words. Some people, to be sure, have no patience with any attempts to clarify meanings. They regard the process as a form of "semantic nit-picking." Such a process can be just that when carried to an extreme. But when initiated as a genuine quest rather than as a method of harassing other people, semantic clarification helps to keep everyone's attention on the subject, and disputation to a minimum.

A third problem—again, previously alluded to (although not in great detail)—is the tendency for statements to be put in "either-or" terms. Among the many reasons why such statements generate arguments is that they are apt to commit us to a more dogmatic view than we really wish to hold. "The government is . . .," "The unions are . . .," "Nixon was. . . ." Sentences that begin this way place a very heavy burden on the speaker, forc-

ing him or her to defend positions that are usually indefensible. We have been told that it is a sign of an open
mind if one can acknowledge that "every issue has two
sides." In my opinion, it is not. It is more likely a sign of
an "either-or" mind. To say that the government, or
Nixon, or America is either this or that grants that there
is another "side" to the issue, but eliminates all the other
possible sides. Or, more precisely, makes it appear as if
two things could not be "true" at one and the same time.
That "America is a racist society" is probably true, but
it is probably also true that America is not a racist society.
It depends on what you want to look at. To impose on
yourself, voluntarily, the total defense of one or the other
position is to aspire to a high and daring form of stupidity.

I would go so far as to say that even the metaphor of
"sides," as in "There are many sides to this issue," is an
expression of a kind of "either-or" thinking. For even if
you conceive of an issue as octagonal, there is the implication that for every side there is its opposite, that if *this*
is true, then *that* cannot be.

There are quite a lot of people who know perfectly well
that one can find many truths in a situation, especially
contradictory ones. But to the extent that they have allowed themselves to talk as if this were not so, they become committed almost against their will to an either-or
conception of events. For example, people who habitually
use the conventional polarities of political discourse—"lib-
eral-conservative," "capitalist-communist," "free world-
unfree world"—find it very difficult to escape from a total
commitment to one "side" or another and cannot acknowledge any weaknesses on their "side." Discussions become
arguments when someone finds himself unable to back

off, to modify, to qualify, and to account for. Either-or sentences do not encourage such multiple-viewpoint thinking.

A fourth reason for a rapid descent from discussion to argument is that our language does not have clear structural markers to distinguish between statements of fact and statements of opinion. The sentences "He is six feet tall" and "He is handsome" look so much alike in their form that it is almost inevitable that we will confuse one with the other at some point in a discussion. Trouble arises for the obvious reason that statements of fact can be verified, whereas opinions cannot. Strictly speaking, you cannot have much of an argument about whether or not someone is six feet tall, assuming, of course, that everyone agrees on what "six feet tall" means, and no one is out to "get" anyone else. There are specific, indisputable ways of determining the answer to everyone's satisfaction. But in the case of "He is handsome," there are no such ways. One can, of course, back up one's opinion with facts, but in the end, an opinion can never be elevated to indisputability.

This need not be a cause of anxiety or melancholy. Most people are perfectly willing to accept the contrary opinions of others, and many an intelligent discussion will end on a note of civil disagreement. Civility begins to depart, however, when opinions come disguised as facts: "Why do you say he's handsome?" "Because he is." The best protection against this form of stupid talk is also the simplest. It requires that you merely signal when you are offering an opinion. You may do so by prefacing your remark with "It seems to me" or "As I see it" or some similar phrase which tells your listeners that you are now talking about yourself, not the "facts" of the case, and that you are well aware of what you are doing. I have found that this procedure rarely fails to keep a conversation from becoming stupid too quickly and will even defuse those who are really bent on arguing. There are, however, some problems with its use. One is that it can become tedious if used almost every other sentence. Another is that it can become "mechanical"—like a twitch or a stammer—and therefore lose its point. I have even come across a case of a man who, upon being asked where he grew up, answered, "It seems to me, Dayton, Ohio."

The point is that what I am suggesting is not a semantic trick or gimmick. It is a serious method of reminding oneself, as well as others, that you have moved from one level of abstraction to another, and from one mode of documentation to another.

I do not want to convey the impression that it is always easy to know the difference between a fact and an opinion. It is possible to maintain, in a serious vein, that all "facts" are only opinions in that none of us can ever say, for sure, how things *are* outside our skins. We are—each of us—wrapped in our protoplasmic containers, and the best we can ever do is say how things look—to us. Reality, Adelbert Ames once remarked, is a perception located somewhere behind the eyes.

Thus, it is not so nonsensical for someone to answer a question about where he grew up with, "It seems to me, Dayton, Ohio." But for our purposes the distinction between fact and opinion can be made in the following way: A "fact" is a statement that refers to observable events (or events that at least once were observable) and is susceptible to verification (or at least once was). You will notice

that in this definition, a factual statement and a true statement are *not* synonymous. By a factual statement I mean
one that is expressed in a form that permits verification or
checking in certain obvious ways (looking, listening,
touching, counting, etc.) and therefore may turn out on
inspection to be false. The statement that "there are 523
pages in this book" is factual in this sense. It is also false.
An opinion, on the other hand, is a bundle of conclusions.
The important point is that it cannot be verified or
checked in the same way that "facts" can. In this respect,
even the statement "He is tall" is an opinion, not a fact.
"Tallness" cannot be verified, since it is a relative term.
What is "tall" to me may not be "tall" to you. But "six foot
three-ness" can be verified in a way that is acceptable to
everyone.

I am not implying, incidentally, that discussions need
to be dominated by factual statements. People's feelings
and conclusions provide just as good material for discussion as facts do. I *am* saying that arguments are likely to
develop when there is confusion about what is offered as
fact and what is offered as opinion.

A frequent instance of this problem is the confusion
between "ought" statements and "is" statements. In fact,
this confusion comes up so often that I will count it, all
by itself, as a fifth cause of argument. The usual way it
develops is that someone asks a question designed to find
out if something *is* the case, or will be. For instance, I recently heard a woman ask what her chances are of getting
employment in a certain field that is male-dominated. The
answer she received was that there is no reason why this
field or any other should not have a healthy proportion
of women.

This is an answer, all right, but not to the question asked. The questioner wanted to know what the situation is; she wanted a *description*. The answerer told her what the situation *ought to be*; she gave her a *prescription*. I have noticed that many people do not make this distinction carefully enough. If you tell them, for example, that such and such a company does not hire women, they will interpret this to mean that you are in favor of such a policy, that in stating what exists, you have stated what ought to exist. That is the sort of reasoning which leads us to punish the messenger when the message is not to our liking.

There is, of course, a certain small validity in this line of reasoning. In looking at any situation, we are apt to select for special attention those aspects of it that will lend support to our general outlook. In other words, we tend to see what we want to see. As a consequence, people who give us the "facts" frequently do so with a barely suppressed smile which says, "That's the way it should be, and I am proving to you that that's the way it is." A man who believes, for example, that American society should offer equal employment opportunity to men and women is apt to offer us facts which show that this is, indeed, being done. But this works the opposite way, as well. There are people who love to give us facts that will demonstrate that what is happening is all wrong, which, of course, they have been saying all along. In other words, a woman who believes in equality may offer us only those facts which show how far we are from the goal.

But granted that there is some connection, sometimes, between what people say is going on and what they want to go on (or what they do not want to go on), it is still necessary to distinguish between description and pre-scription if stupid talk is to be avoided.

A sixth cause of argument is, simply, lack of specificity. In talking about the unions or Italians or Arabs or blacks or students or any other category of people or things, we are, inevitably, taking on more than we can handle. For every statement I can make about "students," you can make one that demonstrates the opposite. This is fairly obvious, and most of us have had ample warning, in school and other places, about the dangers of "overgeneralizing." I mention it here only because I have observed that the warnings have had almost no effect on anybody. Perhaps that is because we have been told in school not to gen-eralize, which would mean the end of all conversation—discussion, argument, or otherwise. The point is that cate-gories have a way of taking charge of conversations in curious ways. For example, the statement "The Italians I work with believe . . ." is not nearly so forceful as "The Italians believe . . . ," and in our desire to be as forceful as we can, we will choose the latter over the former. But limiting the scope of our statements is one of the best ways I know to avoid argument. A statement such as "When I worked at Maher's in 1970, some of the Italians there believed . . ." will almost always receive more cre-dence than one that has not specified where, when, and which.

Finally, it is necessary to include here an important cause of argument—what I judge to be the *second* most feared sentence in the English language. I will not dispute H. Allen Smith's contention that the *first* is "uh, oh," as when a doctor looks at your X-rays and says, "uh, oh." But surely right behind it is the simple declarative sentence,

"I don't know." Perhaps because the penalties for saying it in school are so severe, we have all been conditioned to avoid using it. But I have noticed that almost everyone— physicians, politicians, scholars, garage mechanics (yes, especially mechanics)—will shy away from saying "I don't know" even when that is the most reasonable utterance available to them. You can watch television interviews for years and not hear a single "I don't know," followed by silence. Occasionally, you *will* hear someone say, "I don't know," but it is then followed by, "but I do think that. . . ." In other words, I don't know but I'll tell you anyway. In any case, "I don't know" followed by silence is a marvelous device (especially when you *don't* know) for avoiding stupid talk on all subjects. Contrary to what some people think, it is usually the beginning of intelligent discussions, not the end.

Euphemism

I have previously remarked on two words which, in my opinion, have an undeservedly bad reputation: stereotyping and prejudice (i.e., prejudging). To these, I would like to add a third: euphemism.

A euphemism is commonly defined as an auspicious or exalted term (like "sanitation engineer") that is used in place of a more down-to-earth term (like "garbage man"). People who are partial to euphemisms stand accused of being "phony" or of trying to hide what it is they are really talking about. And there is no doubt that in some situations the accusation is entirely proper. For example, one of the more detestable euphemisms I have come across in recent years is the term "Operation Sunshine," which is the name the U.S. Government gave to some experiments it conducted with the hydrogen bomb in the South Pacific. It is obvious that the government, in choosing this name, was trying to expunge the hideous imagery that the bomb evokes and in so doing committed, as I see it, an immoral act. This sort of process—giving pretty names to essentially ugly realities—is what has given euphemizing such a bad name. And people like George Orwell have done valuable work for all of us in calling attention to how the process works. But there is another side to euphemizing that is worth mentioning, and a few words here in its defense will not be amiss.

To begin with, we must keep in mind that things do not have "real" names, although many people believe that they do. A garbage man is not "really" a "garbage man," any more than he is really a "sanitation engineer." And a pig is not called a "pig" because it is so dirty, nor a shrimp a "shrimp" because it is so small. There are things, and then there are the names of things, and it is considered a fundamental error in all branches of semantics to assume that a name and a thing are one and the same. It is true, of course, that a name is usually so firmly associated with the thing it denotes that it is extremely difficult to separate one from the other. That is why, for example, advertising is so effective. Perfumes are not given names like "Bronx Odor," and an automobile will never be called "The Lumbering Elephant." Shakespeare was only half right in saying that a rose by any other name would smell as sweet. What we call things affects how we will perceive them. It is not only harder to sell someone a "horse mackerel" sandwich than a "tuna fish" sandwich, but even though they are the "same" thing, we are likely to enjoy the taste of the tuna more than that of the horse mackerel. It would appear that human beings almost naturally come to *identify* names with things, which is one of our more fascinating illusions. But there is some substance to this illusion. For if you change the names of things, you change how people will regard them, and that is as good as changing the nature of the thing itself.

Now, all sorts of scoundrels know this perfectly well and can make us love almost anything by getting us to transfer the charm of a name to whatever worthless thing they are promoting. But at the same time and in the same vein, euphemizing is a perfectly intelligent method of generating new and useful ways of perceiving things. The man who wants us to call him a "sanitation engineer" instead of a "garbage man" is hoping we will treat him with more respect than we presently do. He wants us to see that he is of some importance to our society. His euphemism is laughable only if we think that he is not deserving of such notice or respect. The teacher who prefers us to use the term "culturally different children" instead of "slum children" is euphemizing, all right, but is doing it to encourage us to see aspects of a situation that might otherwise not be attended to.

The point I am making is that there is nothing in the process of euphemizing itself that is contemptible. Euphemizing is contemptible when a name makes us see something that is not true or diverts our attention from something that is. The hydrogen bomb kills. There is nothing else that it does. And when you experiment with it, you are trying to find out how widely and well it kills. Therefore, to call such an experiment "Operation Sunshine" is to suggest a purpose for the bomb that simply does not exist. But to call "slum children" "culturally different" is something else. It calls attention, for example, to legitimate reasons why such children might feel alienated from what goes on in school.

I grant that sometimes such euphemizing does not

have the intended effect. It is possible for a teacher to use the term "culturally different" but still be controlled by the term "slum children" (which the teacher may believe is their "real" name). "Old people" may be called "senior citizens," and nothing might change. And "lunatic asylums" may still be filthy, primitive prisons though they are called "mental institutions." Nonetheless, euphemizing may be regarded as one of our more important intellectual resources for creating new perspectives on a subject. The *attempt* to rename "old people" "senior citizens" was obviously motivated by a desire to give them a political identity, which they not only warrant but which may yet have important consequences. In fact, the fate of euphemisms is very hard to predict. A new and seemingly silly name may replace an old one (let us say, "chairperson" for "chairman") and for years no one will think or act any differently because of it. And then, gradually, as people begin to assume that "chairperson" is the "real" and proper name (or "senior citizen" or "tuna fish" or "sanitation engineer"), their attitudes begin to shift, and they will approach things in a slightly different frame of mind. There is a danger, of course, in supposing that a new name can change attitudes quickly or always. There must be some authentic tendency or drift in the culture to lend support to the change, or the name will remain incongruous and may even appear ridiculous. To call a teacher a "facilitator" would be such an example. To eliminate the distinction between "boys" and "girls" by calling them "childpersons" would be another.

But to suppose that such changes never "amount to anything" is to underestimate the power of names. I have been astounded not only by how rapidly the name "blacks" has replaced "Negroes" (a kind of euphemizing in reverse) but also by how significantly perceptions and attitudes have shifted as an accompaniment to the change.

The key idea here is that euphemisms are a means through which a culture may alter its imagery and by so doing subtly change its style, its priorities, and its values. I reject categorically the idea that people who use "earthy" language are speaking more directly or with more authenticity than people who employ euphemisms. Saying that someone is "dead" is not to speak more plainly or honestly than saying he has "passed away." It is, rather, to suggest a different conception of what the event means. To ask where the "shithouse" is, is no more to the point than to ask where the "restroom" is. But in the difference between the two words, there is expressed a vast difference in one's attitude toward privacy and propriety. What I am saying is that the process of euphemizing has no moral content. The moral dimensions are supplied by what the words in question express, what they want us to value and to see. A nation that calls experiments with bombs "Operation Sunshine" is very frightening. On the other hand, a people who call "garbage men" "sanitation engineers" can't be all bad.

Confusing Levels of Abstraction

Many years ago, mathematicians and logicians were confounded by a certain paradox for which their intellectual habits could produce no solutions. The paradox, which had been known about for centuries, is easily stated in the following way: A Cretan says, "All Cretans are liars." If the statement is true, then it is also false (because at least one Cretan, the speaker, has told the truth). We have a proposition, in other words, that is both true and false at the same time, which is terrifying to mathematicians and logicians. Bertrand Russell and Alfred North Whitehead solved this paradox in their great work, published in 1913, *Principia Mathematica*. They called their solution The Theory of Logical Types, and it, also, may be easily stated: A class of things must not be considered a member of that class. Or, to quote Russell and Whitehead, "Whatever involves *all* of a collection must not be one of that collection." And so, a particular statement by one Cretan about all of the statements made by

Cretans is not itself to be considered part of what he is talking about. It is of a different logical type, a different order of things. To confuse them would be like confusing the word *finger* with a finger itself, so that if I asked you to count the number of fingers on your hand, you would (if you were confused) say six—five fingers plus the name of the class of things.

To take another example: There is no paradox in the statement "Never say never" because the first *never* is not at the same level of abstraction as the second, the first never referring to all statements, the second to particular ones.

Now, all of this has made mathematicians and logicians reasonably happy, but what about the rest of us? It does not happen very often, not even on the isle of Crete, that a Cretan will approach anybody and announce, "All Cretans are liars." And as for fingers, not even a deranged logician will say he has six fingers on each hand—five plus the class of things. And yet, for all that, The Theory of Logical Types has some practical implications for reducing our stupid and crazy talk. For one thing, it provides us with a certain awareness of the different types of statements we customarily make. For example, we make statements about things and processes in the world, such as, "The temperature is now ninety degrees." And we make statements about our *reactions* to things and processes in the world, such as, "It is hot." If you think that those two statements are virtually the same, you are on a path that is bound to lead to some interesting stupid talk. Whether or not a thermometer registers ninety degrees is an issue that can be settled by anyone who knows how to read a thermometer. But whether or not something is "hot" depends on who is being heated. To a Laplander, a temperature of fifty-eight degrees may be "hot," to a South African it may be "cold." The statement "It is hot (or cold)" is a statement about what is going on inside one's body. The statement "The temperature is now ninety degrees (or fifty-eight degrees)" is a statement about what is going on outside one's body. Alfred Korzybski provided us with two terms which are useful in talking about these different types of statements: *Extensional* statements are those which try to point to observable processes that are occurring outside our skins. *Intensional* statements are those which point to processes occurring inside our skins.

This distinction is by no means trivial. As I mentioned earlier, more than a few arguments and misunderstandings are generated by people who have confused the two types of statements and who, therefore, look in the wrong direction for verification of what they are saying. I can never prove to a Laplander that fifty-eight degrees is "cool," but I can prove to him that it is fifty-eight degrees. In other words, there is no paradox in two different people's concluding that the weather is both "hot" and "cold" at the same time. As long as they know that each of them is talking about a different reality, their conversation can proceed in a fairly orderly way.

In addition to the differing "horizontal" directions of our statements (inside and outside), there are differing "vertical" directions of our statements. For example, assuming you and I are talking about some event that has occurred, and that we are trying to describe it "objectively," we may still differ in the degree of specificity of our sentences. I may say, "Two vehicles collided." And you may say, "Two Chevy Impalas collided." We are both being extensional in our remarks, but you have included more details than I and, to that extent, come closer to depicting "reality." We may say that my level of abstraction is higher than yours. And as a general rule, the higher the level of abstraction, the less able it is to denote the color and texture and uniqueness of specific realities. I do not say—please note—the less "true" it is. The statement "$E = mc^2$," I am told, is about as "true" as a statement can be, but it is at such a high level of abstraction—it leaves out so many details—as to be virtually useless to all but a select few who use it for specialized purposes. Einstein himself remarked that the more "true" mathematics is, the less it has to do with reality. Nowhere can this be seen more clearly than in our attempts to apply statistical statements to "real" situations. There is, for example, an apocryphal story about a pregnant woman (let us call her Mrs. Green) who went to see her obstetrician in a state of agitation bordering on hysteria. She had read in a magazine that one out of every five babies born in the world is Chinese. She already had given birth to four children and feared that her next would be a victim of the inexorable laws of statistics. The point is that the statement "one out of every five babies in the world is Chinese" is "true," but it is at such a high level of abstraction that it bears no relation to the realities of any *particular* person. It is of a different logical type from any statement made about Mrs. Green's situation and what she, in particular, might expect.

Mrs. Green's problem is apocryphal, but her confusion is not. There are plenty of people who worry themselves to death because they have discovered that they are "below average" in some respect. And there is no shortage of people who falsely assess their own expectations and, indeed, merit, because they have determined they are "above average." For example, a person whose IQ score is "above average" ought not to assume that he or she will have a better chance of understanding a certain situation than a person whose IQ score is "below average." For one thing, a score on a test is a highly abstract statement in itself. For another, a statement about one's score in relation to a thousand other scores is a further abstraction—so far removed from one's performance in a particular situation as to be meaningless. The point is that statistical language of even the most rudimentary sort leaves out so many details that it is, almost literally, not about anything. There is nothing "personal" about it, and therefore it is best to regard it as being of a different logical type from statements about what is actually happening to people.

Generalizations about groups of people present a similar problem. It may be "true," for example, that Jews, as a class of people, have a higher income than Italians, but it does not follow that Al Schwartz, in particular, earns more than Dominick Alfieri, in particular. One of the roots of what may be called prejudice lies somewhere in our confusion over what may be "true" in a general sense and what may be "true" in a particular sense.

The Theory of Logical Types, then, is useful in helping us to sort out our different modalities of talk. There are statements about what we observe and statements about how we feel and statements about our statements (of which self-reflexiveness is an example) and statements about how we classify things—in a phrase, statements about different orders of "reality."

It does not always matter, of course, that we be aware of

these distinctions. No one is more obnoxious than the fanatical semanticist who insists upon straightening everyone out even though they have no wish to be straightened. But, obviously, there are many situations in which people descend into argument, confusion, or despair because they are not aware of the differing types of statements being made. In these cases, knowledge of logical types, levels of abstraction, and extensionality-intensionality can be very useful.

But there is still another application to all of this that is even more useful. I am referring to our efforts at solving problems. The basic distinction that is required here is between "first-order" thinking and "second-order" thinking. (I am lifting these terms from a remarkable book, *Change*, by Paul Watzlawick, John Weakland, and Richard Fisch, in which the authors explain, in great detail, how to apply The Theory of Logical Types to the resolution of practical human problems.) The difference between first- and second-order thinking is a difference in the level of abstraction at which we perceive a problem. When we try to solve a problem through first-order thinking, we work within the framework of the system, accepting the assumptions on which the system is based. For instance, suppose you were given this problem to solve: Here is a number, VI. By the addition of one line, can you make it into a seven? The answer is simple enough—VII. First-order perceptions are entirely adequate for such a problem. But now suppose you are given the following problem: Here is a number, IX. By the addition of one line, can you make it into a six? This problem does not yield to first-order thinking. If you try to solve it by rearranging the elements of the system, you will not come up with a solution. But if you go to another level of abstraction, if you step outside the system, so to speak, an answer suggests itself: SIX. People who cannot solve this problem have usually failed for the following reasons: They assume that IX is a Roman number, and only a Roman number. They assume that the answer must, therefore, be expressed in a Roman number. And they assume that "a line" must be a straight line. In other words, they have "framed" the problem in a certain way and have tried to solve it by staying within that frame. Second-order thinking means going outside the "frame" of a problem and drawing on resources not contained in the original "frame."

There are several different names for second-order thinking. Some have referred to it simply as "creative thinking." The authors of *Change* call it "reframing." Edward de Bono calls it *lateral thinking,* of which he gives the following example:

> There is made in Switzerland a pear brandy in which a whole pear is to be seen within the bottle. How did the pear get into the bottle? The usual guess is that the bottle neck has been closed after the pear has been put into the bottle. Others guess that the bottom of the bottle was added after the pear was inside. It is always assumed that since the pear is a fully grown pear that it must have been placed in the bottle as a fully grown pear. In fact if a branch bearing a tiny bud was inserted through the neck of the bottle then the pear would actually grow within the bottle and there would be no question of how it got inside.
>
> (*Lateral Thinking,* pp. 93 and 94)

One must grant that problems about Roman numbers and pears in bottles are not of the type which ordinarily worry people. But the process by which they are solved— going to another level of perception—can be of substantial practical value. For example, in some New York City public schools, the teachers have a great deal of trouble keeping their students inside the classrooms. Students wander through the hallways during class time, sometimes running, fighting, and screaming, which is not only dangerous but also distracting to those inside the classrooms. Now, if you assume that a classroom is the only place where learning can occur and that those who are not in their classrooms are a "problem," you will spend all your energy trying to get the problems to go where the solution is. You will threaten, plead, and even call the police, none of which works very well. But suppose you "reframe" the problem. Suppose, for example, you say that the issue is not how to get the students into a room but how to get them to learn something. All sorts of possibilities will now become available. In one New York City school, the assistant principal came up with this solution: She announced that the school was instituting a radical educational plan, known as "the open hall policy." The plan made *staying in the halls* a legitimate educational activity. A few teachers were made available to talk with students about a variety of subjects, and thus the halls *became* the classroom. The screaming, running, and fighting stopped, and I have been told on good authority that other principals now visit this school to observe this startling educational innovation.

To take another example, in *Change*, Watzlawick and his associates suggest that people suffering from insomnia will often choose the worst possible path to sleep. They will tell themselves that their problem is "to get to sleep." But since sleep must come spontaneously or it does not come, to work at getting to sleep will defeat its purpose. They recommend a little reverse English: Tell yourself that your problem is to stay awake, and try to do so.

Another example: The New York State Thruway Authority faced the problem of an excessive number of speed-limit violations. They could have, at great expense, hired more troopers to track down the violators. Instead, they raised the speed limit, and thus eliminated much of the problem, with no increase in the accident rate.

The point of all this is that a great deal of stupid talk can be eliminated if we can get beyond and outside of our own assumptions. We too often become tyrannized by the way we have framed a certain situation; that is, we allow a set of words and sentences to define for us the level of perception at which we will view a matter. But if we change our words, we may change the matter. And, therefore, the solution.

Inflation and Mystification

There are two semantic tendencies that are always present when human beings talk, each of which deserves some credit for diminishing the value and clarity of our semantic environments. Both of them are fiercely deplored by writers on the subject of language, who frequently give the impression that the English language itself will collapse unless something is done about them. I doubt it. The English language has been doing very nicely for about a thousand years, and it is a good guess that its future is in no imminent danger. Nonetheless, it is surely worthwhile to call these two tendencies to your attention.

The first is usually called verbal inflation; the second, mystification. Verbal inflation occurs when people broaden the meaning of words to such an extent that it becomes difficult to know what, if anything, the word is supposed to denote. Consider, for example, the word *racist*. There was a time when the word mostly referred to a person holding specific attitudes toward black people—in particular, that they are inferior to whites, and that, therefore, it is best to keep the two races apart. In this sense, Prime Minister Ian Smith of Rhodesia is a racist. There was another more general sense in which the word was applied, namely, to denote any attitude which proceeds from the assumption that "races" of any type differ in important ways and that some "races" are definitely superior to others. In this sense, Joseph Goebbels was a racist.

However, somewhere during the past 20 years or so, the meanings given to this word began to expand rapidly. I distinctly recall hearing John Lindsay being called a *racist* to the applause of many people, because after a New York City snow storm, he had chosen to have the streets of Manhattan cleared but not those of Queens. I have heard Yogi Berra called a *racist* because he used as a pinch hitter Ed Kranepool (a white man hitting .347 at the time) instead of John Milner (a black man hitting .196 at the time). I have been told that anyone opposed to school busing or welfare or the Equal Rights Amendment is a racist. I have heard Daniel Patrick Moynihan, Henry Kissinger, Richard Nixon, Albert Shanker, the entire editorial board of *The New York Times*, and the coaching staff of the Oakland Raiders called *racists* for reasons bearing no discernible connection with each other. What appears to have happened is that the word's meanings have been so stretched that it is hard to tell in what direction to look when the word is used. *Racist* has become a snarl word, roughly synonymous with the sound *ugh!*

In a similar way, the word *super* is in the process of being bloated into uselessness. There are people still living who remember when things came in small, regular, and large sizes. We were then introduced to a "super" size.

And then to a "large super size," followed by an "extra large super size." Presumably, we can expect, soon, a "super extra large super size." I suppose diminishing the size of "super" (or even "large," for that matter) is not especially serious, but inflating the meaning of "friend" is a matter of some consequence. There was a time when a friend was someone you knew for a few years, someone with whom you had experienced some tough and good times, and someone you trusted. But nowadays, TV quiz show "hosts" (what does this do to *host*?) will tell nervous contestants that they have millions of "friends" out there rooting for them. Chase Manhattan Bank is telling us that we have a "friend" in the loan department of every branch. (Does a "friend" lend you money at 12 percent interest?) And, for some people, anyone with whom they have shared a cup of coffee and a danish qualifies as a "friend."

Verbal inflation can be a bothersome problem, depending on which words are getting the treatment. But in general, it is not a process which will cause irreparable damage to either the language itself or important semantic environments. In the first place, it has been going on for a thousand years: Words with precise meanings become words with general meanings become words with no meanings. But usually, if there is a need for some meaning which we once had but have lost, a new word is found to do the job, or perhaps the old word comes back. Karl Menninger recently asked, in the title of one of his books, *Whatever Became of Sin?* I suspect, as I suggested much earlier, that as Americans became more secular in their way of thinking, they substituted *un-American* for *sin*, a fearful loss, in my opinion. But now, as our "faith" in political solutions to problems becomes increasingly unsteady, perhaps *sin* will return. In fact, on the day I wrote these words, there appeared an extraordinary remark in a column written by William Safire of *The New York Times*. In commenting on legislation designed to grant homosexuals equal protection under the law, Safire said that homosexual activity between consenting adults is not (or should not be) illegal. But, he added, it is certainly a sin. For me, at least, the word came roaring off the page. A sin? A real, honest-to-goodness sin? These days, one does not often hear the word used in its theological sense, except perhaps by anti-abortionists. And perhaps the word is best left to pre-twentieth-century eras. I do not argue for or against it here. I say only that if it is badly needed, it is available. The English language is marvelously adaptable. It can supply us with all the words we need in order to conduct our affairs. If we abuse some of our words, we are not therefore on the road to perdition.

Another reason why verbal inflation is not necessarily disastrous is that, except in dictionaries, hard-word lists, and various forms of school tests, words always come to our attention through the mouths and pens of particular people in particular circumstances. We usually have a fairly good idea of how we are to construe a word from the context in which it is used. This means that there are as many different meanings of, say, *friend* as there are circumstances which call forth the word, and most of us are quite capable of supplying an appropriate meaning to a word according to the circumstances of its use. We know, for example, that the Chase Manhattan Bank commercial does not mean by *friend* what we mean by it when we say, "My friend Charlie is coming to town," and we know that "I have a friend in the Mayor's office" means something else still. And that a TV personality referring to his "millions of friends throughout America" also has something else in mind. That is, most of us know this.

In any case, though I think we can survive it, verbal inflation is obviously a tendency that bears careful watching. There is probably a limit (although I don't know where to place it) on just how much inflation our semantic environments can take before their integrity becomes compromised. The important idea about verbal inflation is that as it increases, distinctions become less accessible. A word not only suggests meanings; it excludes other meanings. The more meanings a word is allowed to suggest, the less usable it becomes for precision talking. If we cannot distinguish a "friend" from an "acquaintance," a "right" from a "privilege," a "radical" from a "lunatic," a "conservative" from a "fascist," etc., we are, of course, disarmed.

Though it is also survivable (I think), we ought to be aware of our tendencies toward "mystification." Mystification is a process whereby ideas or events which are perfectly understandable to almost anybody are talked about in such a way that they are inaccessible to all but a select group of people. Although some widely known individuals such as William F. Buckley frequently employ mystification as a style of writing and talking, the main offenders are the practitioners of certain professions. "All professions," G. B. Shaw once said, "are conspiracies against the laity," and nowhere is this charge made more plausible than in the existence of mysterious, technical vocabularies developed by professionals. Here, for example, is a sentence which I found in *The Quarterly Journal of Speech* (Vol. 61, April 1975), written by a man named Leonard C. Hawes, who is, of all things, attempting to develop a theory of communication. The sentence is: "The more familiar experimental approaches resting on a philosophical foundation of logical empiricism complement the less familiar ethnomethodological approaches resting on a philosophical foundation of phenomenology."

A serious reader will suspect, of course, that Mr. Hawes is trying to hide something or perhaps does not quite have a firm hold on what he wants to talk about. But a serious reader could be wrong. Believe it or not, one of the uses of a technical vocabulary is that it is a kind of shorthand. The terms "logical empiricism" and "ethnomethodological" do, in fact, have meanings. Not as precise meanings as the terms of the equation "$E = mc^2$," but ones precise enough that those who are familiar with them can use them without going through elaborate explanations each time they do.

What I mean to imply by this is that while technical terminology can be a "problem"—a source of confusion or deceit—it is not, in my opinion, a *major* one. To be sure, it is the easiest aspect of a vocabulary to parody, and critics who lack character (such as myself) will not fail to do so. I will make amends to Mr. Hawes, therefore, by pointing out that in using such terms, he is not necessarily indicating his confusion, only his exclusiveness. He means to tell us that he is not writing for our understanding but only for those who dwell in his narrow realm. Having landed once or twice in that realm, I can tell you that it is as sterile as Mr. Hawes makes it sound, but it is no crime to be there.

Such linguistic elitism can, however, have serious consequences in situations where it is necessary for the laity to know exactly what is going on.

Here, for instance, is a description of a weekend work-shop offered by the Esalen Institute, which is one of the major centers in the country for the development of Altered States of Stupidity. The workshop is called "Tennis Flow," and it promises to ". . . integrate principles of body awareness, movement, dance, music, and meditation with traditional methods of tennis instruction and practice." So far as I can make any sense out of this piece of mystification, those who enroll in the "workshop" will be playing some tennis and getting a few tips on how to improve their game. The exorbitant fee one must pay for flowing all over the tennis court is made to seem plausible by a word salad of imposing proportions. Of course, we might say that anyone who wants to play tennis and feels the need to go to Esalen for it probably deserves this sort of treatment. But sometimes people get this sort of treatment when they don't deserve it.

Physicians, of course, are notoriously guilty of both mystifying and terrifying patients by using polysyllabic technical terms to denote commonplace and easily curable disorders. In fact, within the past few years, there has grown up a field known as *iatrogenics*. It is essentially the study of how doctor-talk can intensify and even induce illness. Though the term itself is unnecessarily mysterious, the idea of having a field within a field to monitor the harmful consequences of verbal mystification is, in my opinion, a splendid one, and I would urge its replication in every field. Education, for example, is a field with which I am quite familiar, and I can assure anyone who is a member of the laity that there are very few terms employed by educators which cannot be expressed in everyday language and with admirable precision. Therefore, there ought to be a field within the field which is devoted to translating, decoding, or restating in plain language what educators are saying. If there were, educators would probably call it something like *pedagantics*, so that no one would know exactly what it is supposed to do.

In any case, we ought not to underestimate the consequences of mystification in medicine, education, or any other field. One of its principal effects is to make people feel stupid about and alienated from areas of human experience which are exceedingly important to them. Another is to further the notion that if you can *say* a mysterious word or a series of mysterious words, you necessarily know what you are talking about. I have previously said— and will stand by it—that the language of a subject *is* the subject. But there is a difference between *saying* technical words and understanding them. Goethe once remarked that where understanding fails, a word comes to take its place. And that is as good a definition of stupid talk as I have ever heard.

PART

3

Minding
Your Minding

Sometime in 1970, a man had himself admitted to a mental hospital. He assumed a false name and told the doctor who interviewed him a false story—that he heard strange voices that said "empty," "hollow," and "thud." Upon being admitted to the hospital, he proceeded to tell the truth about himself (as best he could and for as long as he was there) to everyone he came in contact with. Seven other people did the same thing in hospitals on the East and West coasts. All of this was part of a three-year "experiment" led by Dr. David L. Rosenhan, a professor of psychology and law at Stanford University.

Dr. Rosenhan claims he was trying to find out if the "sane" can be distinguished from the "insane" in psychiatric hospitals. In an article which appeared in *Science* magazine, he revealed that the "pseudopatients" were not detected at any of the hospitals used in the experiment. Each pseudopatient was discharged with a diagnosis of schizophrenia "in remission," the length of hospital confinement ranging from seven to fifty-two days, with an average of nineteen days. Dr. Rosenhan concluded from all this that the methods of diagnosing "insanity" are not very reliable, and he put forth what appears to him the melancholy view that diagnoses are almost always influenced by the environment and context in which the psychiatrist examines the patient; i.e., the hospital setting predisposes the doctor to assume that a patient is mentally ill.

Naturally. That is the equivalent of saying that if you enter a restaurant, sit down, and call for the menu, the waiter will be predisposed to assume you want to eat. Nonetheless, research is research, and what Dr. Rosenhan seems to have rediscovered are two intertwined principles of human communication which have long been known and which are the basis of much of this book. The first is that the meanings of sentences are not in *sentences* but in *situations*—in the relationship between *what* is said and to whom, by whom, for what purposes, and in what set of circumstances. A psychiatrist sitting at the admissions desk of a "mental hospital" is told by a person who wishes to be admitted that he hears strange voices. What is the psychiatrist supposed to assume? And what are the doctors and nurses in the wards supposed to assume when they speak to the man the next day, or the next week? They will assume that there is "something wrong with him," and that any statement he makes must be viewed in a different light from statements made by a man at a cocktail party or a basketball game. Which leads to the second idea Dr. Rosenhan has stumbled upon. It is the ecological principle of nonadditiveness. If you put a small drop of red ink into a beaker of clear water, you do not end up with a beaker of clear water plus a small drop of red ink. *All* of the water becomes colored. Telling a psychiatrist at a mental hospital that you hear strange voices works in exactly the same way. It changes the coloration of all subsequent statements you are likely to make.

To take another example, a witness who has been caught in one lie to a jury will find it difficult to persuade them that any of his testimony is truthful. Communication, in other words, is not a matter of simple addition—one statement plus another plus another. Every statement we make is limited and controlled by the context established by previous statements. If, on Monday, you insist that you hear strange voices, your denial of this on Tuesday will merely have the effect of confirming that there is "something wrong" with you. All things considered, the "pseudopatients" in Dr. Rosenhan's experiment did pretty well to be released after an average confinement of nineteen days.

But there is still another principle of human communication in this "experiment" which, to this day, Dr. Rosenhan has perhaps failed to uncover. It is the idea that whatever you think is going on in any situation depends on how you "frame" or "label" the event, that is, where you stand in relation to it. For example, Dr. Rosenhan believes that his pseudopatients are "sane" because 1) they did not, in fact, hear any strange voices and 2) they claimed they did only as part of an "experiment." But from another and wider angle, the pseudopatients can be judged to be, if not insane, then at least very curious people. Why, for example, would a "normal" person deliberately have himself committed to a mental hospital? How many people do you know who would even contemplate such an act? And if you knew someone who actually went through with it, you might think that a mental hospital is exactly where he belongs—with or without strange voices. But Dr. Rosenhan and his co-conspirators have legitimized the act—have "sanified" it, if you will—by calling it "an experiment." To them, an experiment is a semantic environment of unimpeachable legitimacy— which is to say, experimenters do not need to explain *their* behavior. Not only that, but Dr. Rosenhan wrote an article about his "experiment" which got published in a prestigious scientific journal. And so, Dr. Rosenhan, his pseudopatients, and the editors of *Science* magazine think they are all quite sane, that patients who *do* hear voices are insane, and that the doctors who labeled the experimenters "schizophrenic" are unreliable. I do not say that they are wrong. But it is just as reasonable to suppose that Dr. Rosenhan and his pseudopatients are strange and unreliable people themselves, and that the doctors in the mental hospitals were entirely competent and judicious. What *Science* magazine should have done is published two articles—one by Dr. Rosenhan about his experiment and another, from a broader perspective, about people who do such experiments and the various labels which might be used to evaluate their behavior. The first article would probably come under the heading of "psychology" (which Dr. Rosenhan is a professor of). The second would come under the heading of "meta-semantics." And it is to "meta-semantics" that I would like to call your attention in this final chapter, for it is the term under which I should like to encapsulate everything in this book.

Meta-semantics is the discipline through which we may make our minds behave themselves. It is the best way I know to regulate and minimize the flow of our own stupid and crazy talk, and to make ourselves less accessible to the stupid and crazy talk of others.

The fundamental strategy of meta-semantics is to put ourselves, psychologically, outside the context of any semantic environment so that we may see it in its entirety, or at least from multiple perspectives. From this position —or variety of positions—it is possible to assess the meaning and quality of talk in relation to the totality of the environment in which it occurs, and with a relatively high degree of detachment. We become less interested in *participating* in semantic environments, more interested in *observing* them.

The move from a participant to a participant-observer position is almost always accompanied by a lessening of fervor, a suspicion of ideology, a willing suspension of belief, and a heightening of interest in the process of communication. For by declining the temptation to attend solely to *what* people are saying, we may focus our attention on the relationships of the *what* to the *whys* and *hows*. Every remark we hear or make is then transformed into a question or a series of questions about its purpose, its tone, its assumptions, its metaphorical structure, its grammatical biases, its conformity to the rules of discourse. Talking or listening to talk changes its character —from a limited reflexive response to a wide-ranging act of inquiry. And inquiry is, and always has been, the most durable and effective antagonist of unwise speech.

But one's will to conduct such inquiries is not summoned easily. Few of us have ever received much encouragement to reflect on the character of the semantic environments we are in. As children, we are educated to respond to *what* is being said to us, not to why and how. Any questions we might be tempted to ask about tone or role-structure or the purposes of a situation are usually disdained—in the home, in school, in church, in the army, in most places. Whatever natural inclinations we might have toward trying to understand "communication as a whole" are dealt with as impertinences, even as threats. We learn soon enough to think fast, not reflectively. The best metaphor I know for this state of affairs is the school examination. Can you imagine a student, upon being handed a test, expressing a desire to discuss the purposes of the test, the assumptions (about people and learning) on which it is based, the metaphors of the mind which are implicit in the form of the test, or the silent questions to which the idea of a test is the answer? The scene is close to unimaginable, but surely the teacher would insist that the student "Get on with it—and fast!" We want people to do what they are supposed to do, say what they are supposed to say, and think, if at all, strictly in the channels assigned to the matter. The rush to do and say, as well as fixed-channel thinking, are the essentials, the catalysts of almost all stupid and crazy talk. Yet the pressures toward them are very good indeed.

I suspect that behind it all is the fear that an excess of awareness will jeopardize the stability and continuity of a situation and thereby destroy it. But this fear, in my opinion, is not well-founded. Consider the case of two people attending a church service. The first knows what she is supposed to do and say but has little awareness of how her behavior is being managed. The second also knows what she is supposed to do and say but, at the same time, knows about how the environment has been designed and is fully aware of its multileveled purposes. She knows about identification reactions and reification and role-structures and fanaticism and all the rest. Will the meaning of the event be the same for both of them? I doubt it. But this does not mean that the second woman will refuse to participate in the event. Knowing that the semantic environment of religion may provide her with a sense of transcendence and her community with a sense of social cohesion, she may be quite willing to do and say exactly what is required of her. But her actions would rest on a foundation of awareness which permits her to be in control of her responses in a way that is not available to the other.

The key idea, then, in meta-semantics is awareness, not cynicism or rejection. To be aware of what is going on in church, in school, in the army, in a sports arena, in a courtroom, in an office, in a laboratory does not imply that you will refuse to do and say what you are supposed to. In fact, the greater one's awareness of the purposes and structures of different semantic environments, the greater is one's sensitivity to the precariousness of all social order, that is, of all communication. To discover that what keeps us together is nothing more substantial than a curious set of symbols and a delicate system of rules is more likely to lead one to humility and conservatism than to iconoclasm and rebelliousness. Shaw's widely known observation that those who worship symbols and those who desecrate them are both idolators captures the sense of what I am trying to say. The man who genuflects without knowing why and the man who spits on the altar both suffer from a lack of control. They are *victims* of a mode of discourse. What we want are not victims but critics, and criticism can be done inside the church as well as out.

However, I am not prepared to argue that awareness of how semantic environments do their work will lead in one direction or another. Among those who have such knowledge, we will find a wide range of attitudes, including reverence, indifference, and skepticism. The point of a meta-sematic view of situations is that it frees us from both ritualistic compliance and reflexive rejection. Once free, we may reenter the situation (or refuse to reenter it) from an entirely different point of view and with a heightened degree of control. Although Dr. Skinner denies it, there can be important differences in levels of consciousness between two people who are doing exactly the same thing. One of them may have the potential to offer reasoned criticism, to modify his own behavior, to resist frivolous change or encourage judicious change, or even to retreat from the environment altogether, in an orderly fashion. The other may be completely dominated by the environment and have no options. And in that difference lies all the difference. For what distinguishes us from other species is not that we can say yes or no (which a dog or a crocodile can do as well), but that we can say yes while reserving the *option* to say no (or vice versa). The distinctively human capability is the provisional response, the critical response, the rational response, the delayed response, the self-conscious response. The meta-semantic response.

And so, positioning ourselves psychologically to inquire into the structure of a semantic environment is a necessary condition to our gaining control over our minding processes. But it is not sufficient. There are two more conditions to be satisfied, and one of them requires that we have some specific questions—an instrument, if you will —with which to make our inquiries. If I have done this book right, most of its previous pages contain explanations of what such questions are. But by way of summary, I have listed below a series of questions which would provide a basis for such inquiries.

What is the general area of discourse I am in? Is this the language of law? science? commerce? religion? romance? education? social lubrication? politics? patriotism? entertainment?

Is there ambiguity or confusion over what sort of situation this is?

How has such confusion been created?

What are the avowed (or hypothetical) purposes of this environment? To satisfy the need for knowledge? for spiritual uplift? for love? for economic security? for social cohesion? for freedom? for protection? for aesthetic pleasure?

What are the purposes that are actually being achieved by the way this environment is organized?

Is there a correspondence between the avowed and actual purposes?

Are there contradictions in purpose between the environment and its subsystems?

Are there conflicts between the purposes (either hypothetical or actual) of the situation and the needs of individuals within the situation? Who *are* the people performing within the situation? How well do they know its rules? How well do they know its language?

What are the general characteristics of the atmosphere of this environment? How are these characteristics made visible? What attitudes are required, and of whom? What is the role-structure of the environment? Is it fixed or fluid? What are the possibilities of changing the atmosphere?

What are the technical terms used in the environment? What are its key terms, including its basic metaphors? Who is controlling the metaphors? Who or what is in charge of maintaining the definitions?

To what extent is the language here characterized by fanaticism? Eichmannism? argument? the IFD disease? by-passing? propaganda? self-reflexiveness? sloganeering? verbal inflation? mystification? euphemism? reification? systemaphilia? confused levels of abstraction? signal reactions? self-fulfilling prophecies? hidden questions? incompatible metaphors? fixed definitions?

What are the effects of any of these "problems"? Do they compromise the integrity of the environment? confuse or otherwise change its purpose? Do they change the atmosphere? Do they change the role-structure? What attitudes do they promote?

Obviously, these are not all the questions that can be asked, and it would not surprise me if I have omitted several important ones. Moreover, these questions are not intended to be asked sequentially. One may begin almost anywhere and will discover that any single question will call forth, eventually, all of the others. The order of the questions will depend on the purposes and priorities of the questioner.

It is also important to say that, in most cases, the questions are extremely difficult to answer. In some instances, it is virtually certain that there will be disagreement even among people who have no great emotional stake in the environment they are analyzing. This is especially true, as I have noted earlier, in the matter of purposes. To me, for example, it seems clear that there is a distinct similarity in the actual purposes (as opposed to the avowed purposes) of such situations as a celebration of the Reverend Moon's Unification Church, a convention of Democratic or Republican governors, and an annual congregation of the *Star Trek* faithful. To you, this similarity may appear strained or even nonexistent. The point is not to achieve consensus on our answers, but on our questions.

Meta-semantic analysis must disappoint you if you are looking for a clean, "objective" assessment of any situation. In the first place, human transactions are so ambiguous and complex, so filled with contradiction and mystery, that it is never possible to say exactly and fully what a situation means. In the second place, the observer must always take into account his or her own disposition. You examine something for a reason, and what your reason is will dictate what you will see and, therefore, say. We see things not as they are, but as *we* are. Even in physics, this principle is accepted. In the subject of human behavior, it holds with even greater force. And so, anything you say about a situation must be modified by the answers to the questions Why am I doing this? What are my own prejudices? How prepared am I to understand what is happening?

In short, we have in the meta-semantic questions neither

a catechism nor an exact science, but a kind of multi-pointed compass which directs where we shall look but not what we shall see.

Assuming, then, that this list of questions is a reasonably useful guide to inquiry, the meta-semantic view would require still another, a final, step if it is to help us gain control over our minding processes—namely, the making of *judgments* about what people (including ourselves) are saying. And here we enter the inescapable realm of *values*. In exploring that realm, I want to begin by restating the ways in which I have defined stupid talk and crazy talk.

I have said, first of all, that both stupid talk and crazy talk are *evaluations* made by particular people. This may be obvious enough, but to keep well clear of reification, I want to stress one more time that stupidity and craziness are not *in* the sentences we speak or hear, or even *in* situations. They are *judgments* one makes about the relationship of talk to the totality of the situation within which talking occurs. This implies that the justification for any judgment rests, ultimately, on the judge's conception of what is workable or what is desirable. And in these two terms—workable and desirable—we have the basis of the distinction I have tried to make between stupid and crazy talk. It is, I believe, a distinction worth making since their consequences for the maintenance of healthy semantic environments are quite different, and therefore, we are required to deal differently with them. Stupid talk, I have argued, is talk that does not do what it is supposed to do (according to you). It is talk (according to you) that misconstrues the atmosphere of a semantic environment or is not aware of its motivating questions or projects metaphors that are incompatible with those of others in a situation or misinterprets a role-structure or, through self-reflexiveness, goes far beyond any reasonable chance of clarifying an issue. Stupid talk is talk whose purpose is legitimate (according to you), but whose character is not. Its fault is that it does not work, or cannot work.

Moreover, stupid talk tends to be an individual aberration. It is, so to speak, a mistake one makes in the give-and-take of talking. It may even be a mistake one makes repeatedly, but it is usually not the sort of thing one *wants* to do. And that is why stupid talk is frequently fairly easy to correct. If the corrector and the correctee (who may be the same person) share roughly the same understanding of the purposes of a semantic environment, they are likely to have an amiable meeting of minds. It is as if someone wants to drive from New York to Chicago in the fastest possible way and to accomplish this end has arranged to drive through New Orleans. Assuming that you and he can agree on what *fastest possible way* means, what *Chicago* means, and that Chicago is a desirable place to go, your efforts to improve his performance ought to be well-received. Of course, if you do not agree on these things, you have another kind of problem, which we will come to presently. But what I am trying to say here is that stupid talk tends to be an individual, pragmatic issue. The question it involves is whether or not what has been said will achieve its purposes within the framework of a generally accepted semantic environment.

I do not, incidentally, wish to imply that the question of "workability" is always an easy matter to decide. Reasonable people will often differ on whether or not something has worked, or, if agreeing on that, will disagree on why. But observation of actual effects will frequently lead the way out of such dilemmas. After all, talking is a hypothesis, a prediction, an experiment, and, therefore, to some extent, its success or failure can be verified. If I wish to sell you a car, I will try to do it by a certain kind of talk. If you do not buy, and if enough others do not buy, I have a basis for assuming that my talk is implicated in my defeats. Stupid talk, in other words, is an individual's failed experiment. The experiment may have involved an attempt to sell a car, to amuse, to discover a fact, to create a sense of reverence, or to help someone see something more clearly. But in most cases, there are *effects* to be observed, and we may find enlightenment by rigorously attending to them. Unless, of course, we are enraged or feeling especially vulnerable. Or unless certain habits of speech have become so lovable, so deeply ingratiating to our personalities, that rather than change them we would choose to live with ambiguity, confusion, and ineffectiveness. All of us, in some measure, are so afflicted: We are stupid-talk junkies. At least so far as one or two semantic environments are concerned.

I know people whose ability to use the language of commerce is comprehensive and acute. They know virtually everything about it: its purposes, tone, roles, metaphors, technical terms. Nothing escapes their notice, especially unanticipated consequences. And yet, as they move from business situations to, say, politics or religion, their understanding diminishes in quantum leaps. They do not know what they are saying or what others are saying to them. They do not even know what is expected of them. But, curiously, they do not seek improvement. They *enjoy* their stupid talk, as we all do in one situation or another.

I know of no remedy for the enjoyment of stupid talk except to wait until the observable effects of such talk become an intolerable burden. In which case, it may be too late. Our stupid talk may have become transmuted into crazy talk.

Crazy talk is almost always endearing to those who use it, and observations of its effects will on no account influence its direction. Crazy talk occurs when we do not agree on where Chicago is or, especially, on whether or not one should go there altogether. The question of the effectiveness of crazy talk is not relevant. Crazy talk may or may not work. Its fault is that (from your point of view) its purposes, definitions, tone, and metaphors are loathsome or destructive or evil or even overwhelmingly trivial. As a consequence, there is no way of which I am aware that you can prove, demonstrate, or even explain to another that he is talking crazy. For example, consider Yasir Arafat's observation that the Palestine Liberation Organization "does not want to destroy any people. It is precisely because we have been advocating coexistence that we have shed so much blood." Here we are not dealing with an aberrant, improvable remark. We are confronted by an aberrant pattern of thought of a type that frequently takes possession of men who have been in war too long (as must have also been the case of the U.S. officer in Vietnam who said that "We destroyed the town in order to save it."). In fact, Arafat's "enemy," Moshe Dayan, who has also been in war too long, gave an entirely new meaning to both the Western and Eastern conceptions of logic in commenting on the shooting down of a Libyan airliner. He said that, technically speaking, Israeli planes did not shoot it down but merely knocked off one of its wings. Judges of the world should take note, for here is an entirely new line of defense against any charge of homicide!

One may argue that Arafat and Dayan are speaking this way only to reduce hostile political opinion toward their respective causes, but that they would choose such language in order to achieve this reflects a conception of political discourse that is entirely deformed (according to me). And if it does not appear so to many others, that is exactly the point I am leading to. Crazy talk is not, by and large, an individual departure from reason. It reflects a collective point of view. It is talk for which there is a large and favorable audience. It puts forward a conception of purpose and tone and value that is embodied in a philosophy or a movement or an ideology. In an earlier chapter, I quoted from the terse speech given by Nazi guards to the newly arrived inmates at a concentration camp. The remarks were designed to reduce the chances of rebellion among the inmates, and, as far as I know, were effective in doing so. Hardly stupid talk. But the basic purpose of the concentration camp was to kill people, and for no other reason than that they were of a different "race" from the killers. There were many people to whom this made perfectly good sense, as there are many people today to whom killing for peace makes good sense.

To me, this is crazy talk. If someone else does not agree, he and I are at an impasse. We have reached the final frontier of semantic analysis. There is nothing left to say except I believe this and you believe that. Therefore, the meta-semantic view requires that the judgment of crazy talk be placed in a fairly clear value context. It cannot be cloaked as science or scholarship or even informed opinion. To say that something is crazy talk is to impugn some-one's concept of reality, to challenge his values, to deny the legitimacy of his purposes. In doing so, we are using the language of religion, in its purest sense. We assert what is desirable, but we cannot prove it.

Therefore, I wish to reiterate some of the most impor-tant values on which I base my judgments of crazy talk. These, as well as several others, have no doubt already made themselves visible to you throughout the book, espe-cially in the examples I have provided. But it is an essen-tial part of the meta-semantic view that the judge use every means available, including redundancy and gen-eralities (as well as examples), to make known the pref-erences on which his judgments are based.

I begin, then, by noting that in the questions I have put forward as instruments of inquiry, there are several im-plicit values. Foremost among these is the value of inquiry itself. I take it as given that any talk which actively tries to discourage inquiry about itself is crazy talk. For exam-ple, I was recently sent a piece of advertising for the group known as est, to which I have previously alluded. The advertisement explains, in question and answer form, the ways of knowing promoted by est. One of the questions is, "Will I have to take notes or study anything?" The an-swer is as follows: "No, est is an experience; there is noth-ing to study . . . nothing to remember, nothing to figure out." This kind of talk strikes me, on the face of it, as crazy. I have long assumed that what is most worthwhile about our species is that we can study, remember, and figure out better than all the others, with the possible exception of the hump-backed whale. To refrain from exercising this talent, therefore, appears to me to diminish our humanity, and any system of speech which encourages us to be less human is crazy talk.

I do, however, acknowledge, as I have stated several times earlier, that there are a few well-established semantic environments—love-making, for example—where an excess of inquiry behavior can be ruinous to an understanding and appreciation of the event. But even there, one may think *before* the event and *after* the event and thereby predict and evaluate its consequences to one's life. There are lovers and then there are rapists, and the difference lies in how one studies, remembers, and figures out the encounter. From all of this you will understand that I am placing the highest possible worth on the *process* by which people come to their conclusions. It has lately been claimed that of the two hemispheres of the brain, the one on the left is largely in control of our capacity to analyze, to employ logic, and to apply principles—indeed, to use language itself. Semantic environments which are designed to suppress or by-pass the functions of the left hemisphere of the brain, even if they are disguised as therapies, are therefore highly suspect (in my scheme of things) and are likely to produce large quantities of crazy talk.

You may also have gathered from what has gone on before that I place a high value on social order and its four pillars—empathy, tradition, responsibility, and civility. I realize that these words are extremely abstract and therefore not easy to define. I am using them here to suggest the socially conservative idea that there is something worth preserving in most semantic environments. What I have been calling "semantic environments" are, after all, situations shaped by long human experience, and their purposes and language are on no account to be taken lightly or to be revised precipitately. Those who are quickest to call for a reordering of some social system, including its language, are usually those who are most insensible to how much they, themselves, depend on conventional rules and roles. Nothing could be more ridiculous, for example, than a person who accuses the police of brutality, calls for a People's Army to replace them, and then is astonished at being smacked by a policeman's billy club.

We are bound together by thousands of unwritten contracts without which we would lose the entire basis of predictable continuity in life. And there is a certain craziness in any talk that places such continuity in jeopardy. In a fundamental sense, there may be nothing crazier than the philosophy which advocates "doing your own thing." For in the sense in which it is sometimes meant, the phrase implies a releasing of oneself from social contracts, including semantic restraints and rules. But, again, those who are most passionate about doing their own thing do not normally expect a bus driver to do *his* own thing, which may be to take the Third Avenue bus to Tenafly, New Jersey, to visit his girl friend.

And so, there are forms of crazy talk (according to me) which consistently come from systemaphiles, utopians, and revolutionaries—people who do not sufficiently appreciate the delicate ecological balance by which semantic environments maintain their usefulness. You might call such people "the book burners," no matter what their philosophy. They are driven by the desire to erase tradition, to unburden us, all at once, of the weight of human experience. But book burning is not a form of literary criticism. It is not a form of criticism at all. It is a form of crazy talk.

On the other hand, nothing could be more obvious than that our semantic environments are in need of modification. Therefore, the fanatics and Eichmanns among us will provide a constant source of crazy talk "defending the indefensible," never questioning purposes, and thereby refusing to allow for change. They are the mirror images of the book burners, because neither appreciates the need for continuity; the book burners disdain what is past, the Eichmanns what is ahead, fearing all those modifications of purpose, tone, metaphor, and role that keep a semantic environment responsive to human needs. In summary, I am saying that crazy talk is characterized by patterns of thought which reveal an unwillingness to inquire, an exorbitant disdain for tradition, and a paralyzing fear of change.

To these, I must add the following two ideas (values). First, that crazy talk is extremely likely to emerge when there is a failure to differentiate carefully among semantic environments. As Karl Kraus long ago remarked, there is a difference between a chamber pot and an urn. And one might say that crazy talk is a consequence of not knowing the difference, as when (for example) the language of athletic competition is confused with the language of patriotism. My sense of my country's worth is not enlarged because an American rowing crew beats some Peruvians in the Olympics. Nor is it diminished if the Peruvians win. Talk to the contrary strikes me as crazy.

To take another example: When I vote for a presidential candidate, I do not assume that this is what God wanted me and everyone else to do. And those who assume so are, according to me, talking crazy. I do not look to astrology to provide me with a basis for predicting the future. And I do not look to science to tell me where my loyalties should lie. I do not believe that schools ought to be political organizations. And I do not believe that political organizations should function as advertising agencies. People who talk as if their religion were a political party and as if commerce were a religion, marriage a court of law, a court of law a sporting event, a sporting event a form of patriotism, patriotism a form of family life, usually project a vision of reality that I find crazy. If an individual or a society cannot distinguish between the uses of a chamber pot and the uses of an urn, then neither will have any clear conception of how to behave.

Finally, I must avow my belief that the best defense against all varieties of crazy talk is our old friend a sense of humor, which is always available as an escort through hard and confusing times. I mean by a sense of humor an active appreciation of the fact that time's winged chariot is always at our backs and that therefore there is a profound and essential foolishness, transiency, and ineptitude to all our adventures, including the hardest of all, talking to each other. Without a sense of humor, almost any talk will, soon or late, descend into craziness, brought down by its own unrelieved gravity. I believe that a sense of humor is at the core of all our humane impulses, and he who would make us mad must first exorcise our appreciation of human frailty, which is what a sense of humor is.

A person with a sense of humor will not say, unless with irony, that we can kill for peace or that break-in men are guilty of an excess of zeal or that you are perfect the way you are, which is what Voltaire said in *Candide*, laughing all the way. A person with a sense of humor will not say that a marriage contract should specify when the dishes are to be done and by whom or that God wants us to show the world that Americans can compete with the Russians. A person with a sense of humor will not shout *Sieg Heil* or seriously believe that any idea is infallible. And a person with a sense of humor will hardly try to sell you a car by persuading you that in buying it, you will enter the Kingdom of Heaven.

And so, it comes down to this: The management of our minding is a Sisyphean task. We can never finish doing it. We can only keep pushing the rock, armed with what William James called the feeblest force in nature, our capacity to reason. The temptations to subvert that capacity are attractive and persuasive. Everywhere, it seems, we are advised to relax, to empty our minds of thought, to be spontaneous, to avoid being uptight, and to believe the unbelievable. This is the age, I am told, of Transcendental Meditation. I rather think it is the moment, not the age. At least, I hope so. For each day, the devils of crazy and stupid talk awake when we do, eager to mismanage our affairs. Their only antagonist is Reason, and they will give way to Rational Meditation, and no other.

An Autobibliography

The inclusion of a bibliography at the tail end of a book is one of the more benign pieces of stupid talk practiced by authors. The ritual has only one of two possible purposes, neither of which is usually accomplished. The avowed purpose is to provide a reader with additional sources of information about the subject of the book. But most times, so many books are cited and in such an undifferentiated and imperious way that the reader does not know where to begin or how, and so wisely decides to ignore the whole matter.

Of course, the actual purpose of the bibliography is to impress the reader with the extent of the author's learning. This, too, is often a waste of effort, since the reader, having come to the end of the author's own book, has already decided if the author is a person of intellectual substance. If the decision is affirmative, then the bibliography is unnecessary. If negative, then the bibliography is insufficient.

With all of this in mind, I present below my "autobibliography": a brief, highly personal commentary on nine books from which I have learned a great deal. I do not claim they are great books or seminal books or indispensable books, only that after I read them, I felt a lot smarter than before. I recommend them to your attention.

The first is Alfred Korzybski's *Science and Sanity* (The International Non-Aristotelian Library Publishing Company, 1933). This is, in fact, one of the worst books ever written. The book is messy in every respect, and it is painfully obvious that many of the subjects Korzybski discusses were well beyond his range. It is also impossible to read for more than five pages at a sitting, especially if you have tendencies toward migraine. If you think of a book as a container of answers, you will hate *Science and Sanity*. But if you think of a book as an instrument for the stimulation of thought, you should find Korzybski unforgettable. He addresses himself to questions of profound interest (at least to me). For example, what are the characteristics of language which lead people into making false evaluations of the world around them? He also tries to say how we may avoid talking excessively crazy. Many academicians do not care for Korzybski—in part, because he is not careful, and in part, because they have no patience with genius.

The second book is *Mind, Self, and Society* by George Herbert Mead (University of Chicago Press, 1934). This, too, is a badly written book, repetitious and abstract. In fact, Mead did not even write the book. It was put together by students of his from notes made at Mead's lectures. Nonetheless, in my opinion, there does not exist anywhere a better description of how meanings are made and, therefore, of how communication becomes possible. Mead, incidentally, was one of the founders of social psychology, American variety, and it is from him that the concept of a semantic environment comes.

The third book is *A Critique of the New Commonplaces* by Jacques Ellul (Alfred A. Knopf, 1968). Ellul is a professor of the history of law and social history at Bordeaux and is one of the world's best authorities on stupid and crazy talk. I got the idea for my book after reading *Commonplaces*, in which Ellul analyzes more than thirty slogans that are popularly and uncritically used by intellectuals and other varieties of gurus. One of them is, "The main thing is to be sincere with yourself." Another is, "Cultivate your personality: be a person!" If you think these slogans are good advice, you ought to read Ellul to get a different perspective on them, and almost anything else you believe.

The fourth book is *The Collected Essays, Journalism and Letters of George Orwell* (Harcourt, Brace, and World, 1968). Actually, almost anything by George Orwell has been valuable to me because he is the most clearheaded thinker I know. He is never tyrannized or even captivated by words, and his analyses of the way people's minds become unsettled by nonsense are the best examples we have of "crap detecting." My ambition in life is to grow up to be George Orwell.

258 CRAZY TALK, STUPID TALK

The fifth book is Wendell Johnson's *People in Quandaries* (Harper, 1946), which is a gentle, beautifully written, entirely intelligible popularization of Korzybski's ideas. I am tempted to say that there are two kinds of people in the world—those who will learn something from this book and those who will not. The best blessing I can give you is to wish that as you go through life you should be surrounded by the former and neglected by the latter.

The sixth book is *Rules for Radicals* by Saul Alinsky (Random House, 1971). Alinsky made a distinguished career by helping people to organize themselves in order to further their own economic and political interests. His book is a tough-minded and accurate description of what people need to know about communication in order to achieve their purposes. Alinsky is almost never likable but is so smart that he compels you to stay with him.

The seventh book is Karl Popper's *The Open Society and Its Enemies* (Princeton University Press, 1963). Popper is a professor emeritus at the London School of Economics and a world authority on the philosophy and history of science. This book is scholarly and not recommended for casual summer reading. But it is the most brilliant discussion of the roots of fanaticism I know of. When I have depressing days, weighted down by excessive exposure to crazy talk, it helps me to get through if I remind myself that Karl Popper is alive and *thinking* in England.

The eighth book is I. A. Richards' *Practical Criticism* (A Harvest Book, 1956). This book appears on the surface to be about poetry and how people respond to it. But it also puts forward a general theory of communication and identifies many of the "faults and errors" by which understanding is thwarted. Although Richards is not a good writer, he knows (in my opinion) more about the languaging process than anyone alive, and I have never failed to learn something important from any of his books.

The ninth book is Gregory Bateson's *Steps to an Ecology of Mind* (Ballantine, 1972). This book is well-written and brilliant but strange. Bateson is no respecter of academic conventions and, here, allows himself to go wherever his ideas take him. He is, incidentally, the inventor of the Double Bind Theory of schizophrenia and a strong advocate of the idea that "craziness" is a product of a disordered communication pattern.

Finally, at the risk of sounding pretentious, I want to mention that once a year I reread six writers who were devoted (each in his peculiar way) to the detection of humbug. They are Jonathan Swift, Thomas Jefferson, Thomas Paine, George Bernard Shaw, Alfred N. Whitehead, and Bertrand Russell. Like the rest of us, they are not without fault and are certainly guilty, now and then, of both stupid and crazy talk. But they have the great merit that they never doubted that men are capable of saying a few reasonable words each day.

Index

266 INDEX

What-do-you-mean? question, 153–56

Whatever Became of Sin? (Menninger), 224

Whitehead, Alfred North, 213, 256

Wittgenstein, Ludwig, 6, 55

Women's Liberation Movement, 65–66

Words, 100, 242; idealized, 119–20; "key," 61–63; 144–45; and meaning, 156–57; metaphors, 63–67; mystification of, 226–29; as subject, 54–56, 135–42; technical, 53–61, 226–27; and types of sentences, 67–70; verbal inflation of, 222–26

Wouk, Herman, 72, 79

Yourinko, Mr. and Mrs. Joseph, 108

Ziegler, Mel, 83–86